TIMELESS SISTERS

Peace at the River

Shelly Hoover

CONTENTS

In gratitude to the sisterhood of women who have come before me and those who walk alongside me, this story is dedicated to those celebrating or searching for their tribe.

THE TALISMAN

Each suffers alone. Yet, the path to community is but a step away. The talisman, passed down the maternal line, is the key to unlocking the portal to the healing power of sisterhood. Follow the stories of Janene, a modern-day high school teacher; Cora, a young slave during the Civil War; and Amadahy (ama-day-he), a Cherokee from the 1600s. Three timeless sisters who meet, searching for peace at the river.

CHAPTER ONE

Janene

Durham, North Carolina
2014

Bad news travels at the speed of light.
– Tracy Morgan

I'd known since the accident that something was terribly wrong. In April, the neurologist said it was possible. Today, my husband Tom and I waited to hear the specialist's opinion at Duke University. How did I, a healthy 47-year-old woman, end up here? My body had betrayed me. Looking to Tom for support, I saw his jaw muscles tighten rhythmically, his unconscious manifestation of stress. Cutting through the expectant tension, we exchanged concerned glances and looked away. Ten months of fruitless medical tests and a thousand Internet searches would be resolved when one doctor came through the door.

Ten months prior in Westbrook, North Carolina

Tom and I were on a morning run through the neighborhood.

Red maples blossomed along familiar streets. Abandoned bikes and basketballs adorned manicured lawns. Time we enjoyed together nurtured our relationship amid busy lives. We'd moved here 24 years ago when I began teaching at Westbrook High. Westbrook, a small community, nestled in lavender meadows and the Aguaquiri River, was an ideal place to raise our family.

"Pick up your feet, Janene. They're dragging."

Tom cautioned me. Despite the warning, with the next step, my toe caught the asphalt. My left hand broke my fall as I tucked and rolled on the street like an armadillo seeking cover. Tom ran over and knelt next to me, looking for signs of injury.

"Are you okay?" Tom caressed my arm. "Can you sit up?" He supported my back with one hand and pulled me upright with the other.

"What the...?" I said to no one in particular and surveyed the damage by the predawn light. Shaken, I anticipated road rash and bruises. My shoulder throbbed, and my knees bled. Asphalt pebbles embedded themselves in the palm of my hand.

"I'll be all right." I stood up, brushed off the dirt and embarrassment, and tried to jog the half-mile home. I gave up after a few steps, not realizing I'd never run again. Tom and I walked home as the mockingbirds sang a morning song, and the sunrise peeked over the horizon.

"Have a seat," Tom said as he guided me to the couch. "I'll get some ice."

"Tylenol and coffee, too, please."

I propped my feet on the ottoman, leaned back, and examined the palm of my hand. "Ow!" I inhaled through my teeth as I picked at the pebbles that had hitched a ride.

As newlyweds, our four-bedroom house seemed like a mansion. Empty rooms awaited children, and sand-colored carpeting anticipated the tide of toys. Over time, hardwood covered the floors, and leather sofas replaced Grandma's old davenport. A warm, Tuscan palette replaced the 90's pastel interior, and granite countertops won over square tiles and grout. Tom, the

DIY aficionado, made it happen.

"Where do you want the ice?"

"Left shoulder and across my knees."

I sipped enough coffee to get the Tylenol down.

"That's going to hurt for a few days," Tom said.

"I'll survive. Just need to shower off the sweat and street." I adjusted the ice bags and contemplated the start of the coming school year. I spent the end of summer vacation nursing my wounds and fretting over lesson plans.

The first day back to work, I walked into the school office, trying to mask my hobbled gait. Pine scent signaled the fresh start to a new year. "Hi, Gloria!" I smiled and waved my bandaged hand. "How's my favorite Wolf?" I handed Gloria an iced chai latte and a bouquet of flowering dogwood, her favorites.

Gloria ran the school office, advocating for students yet enabling none. Her once silky, black ponytail turned to a silver crown since she had taken me under her wing. Wolves of every shape and size adorned her cubicle, resin statues of predators on the hunt or howling at the moon and a she-wolf protecting her pups.

One wolf, in particular, stood watch above the rest, a painting that belonged in a history museum. The valiant white wolf stood alongside a Cherokee woman. Was he a partner or protector? Fine strokes of oil paint detailed the wolf's dense fur; silver flecks drew light to its sapphire eyes. Long copper and golden brown brush strokes traced the woman's lean muscle. Dark eyes surveyed the landscape through ceremonial red face paint. Jet black hair appeared to wave in the breeze, framing her regal profile. What did she see? What did she feel? What did she dream about behind those obsidian eyes? I felt a spiritual connection to her, confirmed by a shiver down my spine.

Gloria sprang to greet me, and our embrace lingered.

"What on earth happened?" Gloria asked, looking at my hand.

"It's no big deal. I tripped during a morning run."

"I'm sorry, dear." Gloria furrowed her brow as she sensed my deceit. "How was your summer, Janene?"

"Hannah and I enjoyed an east coast college tour. Tom and Daniel spent most of the summer at the Hiwassee Reservoir. Tom is proud of his new fishing boat. What about you? How are your adorable grandbabies?"

Gloria smiled as her grandchildren came to mind. "We spent time together on the coast. They're growing too fast for me. Miya will be a freshman this year, hard to believe. Get ready, sweetheart." Gloria returned to her desk and patted a stack of folders. "The Wolves return tomorrow."

I walked to my classroom, hoping the musty smell had abated. It smelled of dusty books and sweaty teens when I'd left it last June. I'd been walking through locker-lined hallways and up and down the worn marble stairs to Room 210 for years and never remembered it to be a burden. The burn emanating from my hips caused me to pause midway and grab the stair rail. It must have been a result of my fall. I pushed through the pain and reached classroom 210, my second home.

When school started the following day, I'd begin with 11th graders in AP United States History. The north and east classroom walls depicted the life of the Cherokee people in Aguaquiri, now called the Qualla Boundary. That's Western North Carolina before the Eastern Band of Cherokee purchased their own land from the federal government rather than be forced westward on the Trail of Tears. My remaining four classes were 11th and 12th graders in American History I. The south and west classroom walls highlighted the social, political, economic, and cultural history of America during the Civil War. I felt alive while engaging students in our history.

My chest lifted as I drew a deep breath in anticipation of seeing fresh faces in the morning. That reminded me to review my class roster flashcards. I printed out my students' photos, taped them to index cards, and wrote their names on the back. I studied the cards and challenged myself to greet each student by name on the first day of class. I expected my students to put forth their best efforts in my class, and I wanted to show them

I did my homework too. I remembered 160 of the 185 students' names. That's a solid B performance, so I had more work to do.

I awoke in the morning to the sound of cascading water and longed to linger in bed with my cozy 800 thread count sheets. My bedroom provided sanctuary from those in need of my constant attention. A generous row of windows framed silverbell and holly trees that grew in the backyard. Yet, the prospect of seeing my students drew me out of bed. My once strong and agile legs felt encased in concrete. I hurled them over the side of the bed and stood up. I took one step and crumpled to the floor. Tom came running from the bathroom with a towel wrapped around his middle-aged waist.

"Are you alright, honey?"

"I think so, my legs just gave out on me."

I got to my hands and knees and grabbed Tom's hand to help me up.

"I'm worried about you. You've got to get this checked out."

"I've been off lately, but I'll be fine."

What a strange feeling. My body had never failed me like this before. I tried to explain away the fatigue with the fact that teaching is exhausting work, both physically and emotionally. But it was never this exhausting and school hadn't started. I put on my tattered, white robe, and made my way to the kitchen.

"Good morning, Hannah. Is Daniel up?"

"Yeah, I heard him in the shower."

Hannah pulled her thick brown hair across the crown of her head so it wouldn't fall in her oatmeal.

"Have you talked to him lately?" I asked.

"A little. He's been busy."

"What's been going on?"

"Just the usual, I guess."

My daughter Hannah, being three years older, acted as a second mom to her brother, Daniel. I adored them both, yet lately, I couldn't connect with Daniel as I had in the past. Teenage angst interfered. He spent time with his phone and friends as typical 14-year-old kids do. Hannah was an amiable daughter and did well in school. She knew early on that she wanted to be an archaeologist or anthropologist. I'd like to think that I have influenced her with my passion for peoples of the past. My thoughts wandered back to my physical mystery. I'd prefer to press on and get through this without a doctor. But to honor Tom's request, I decided to make an appointment with my nurse practitioner.

I grabbed a banana and returned to my bedroom to get ready for work. Tom was dressed in a t-shirt and shorts, prepared for the commute to his home office down the hall.

"I've got a meeting this morning. Have a good day." Tom kissed me on the forehead and left the bedroom, coffee in hand.

I stepped into the shower and visualized the hot water, washing away my concerns. I perused my wardrobe, looking for something comfortable to wear. A Wolfpack gray and blue blouse and stretch jeans worked for me. I walked to the garage and noticed that Tom's boat, Ruby Tuesday, was covered, a sign of the season's end. I slid into my blue Camry, a familiar comfort. A new three-ring binder, titled Engaging Today's Youth, lay on the passenger seat. I needed to add this to my bookshelf of unused professional development binders. I gathered empty coffee cups and protein bar wrappers, a symbolic clean start to a new school year, and an illusion that I'm in control.

Without warning, my back muscles seized, and I sank into the driver's seat. Like a rogue wave, panic rushed through me from head to toe. I gulped for air as my throat constricted. Was it a panic attack? Breathe. Breathe. Just breathe. My mind perseverated -- Daniel playing football, Hannah driving, my students learning, the potholes destroying Main Street, the duration of red lights. Breathe.

A similar feeling surfaced from my distant memory. A car crashing through my bedroom window haunted my childhood dreams. I survived, but my dollhouse family lay broken in pieces, immutable faces staring at me. I fell to my knees and gathered their scattered body parts, bloodied torsos, arms, and legs. I frantically tried and failed to put the dolls back together.

The eyes, painted on bodiless heads, stared with disappointment and disdain. I held the body parts in clenched fists and awoke to the sound of my own scream.

I shook my head to brush off the craziness. I can do this. Start the car. Focus. I backed the car onto the street and began the familiar drive to school. I drove down Riparian Way and thought about my neighbors as I passed by their homes. I wondered how Lisa was recovering from her mastectomy. I needed to bring her dinner. What about Nancy's son, my former student Justin? I heard he is home from Afghanistan. I'd been a terrible neighbor lately and made a mental note to check in on my friends.

I pulled onto Main Street with a renewed sense of determination. I can handle this. It's just my legs being wonky. This too, shall pass. I attempted to rein in my thoughts. Cars parked in Olsen's used car lot reflected the morning sun. Customers stood in line at Woody's Donuts. The maple bars were worth the wait.

The stoplight ahead shone red, and my leg was supposed to move to the brake pedal without a thought. Instead, it stiffened into a painful spasm and hit the gas pedal. My world went into slow motion as I swerved to avoid ramming into the UPS truck in front of me. I felt my cheeks bounce, and my body flail like a rag doll as my car jumped the curb. The sounds of screeching metal and shattering glass succumbed to silence.

I awoke to the sounds of mechanical whirring and buzzing. I flirted with consciousness in an aura of claustrophobia and attempted to look around to make sense of my surroundings. An unfamiliar voice boomed over a speaker.

"Mrs. Branch, please hold still, or we will have to begin the CT scan again. Hang in there; we're almost done."

Blurry gray and white images faded until I was out again. I had visions of falling while family and friends reached out to save me. I'd grab someone's hand and slip away. I felt as though no one could reach me, no matter how hard they tried. I grew weaker as I fell. I couldn't move, I couldn't scream. I had no air to breathe. I regained consciousness, unable to see past the bright light. The clamor of the CT subsided, and I felt a familiar hand on mine.

"Tom? Is that you?"

"Yes, honey. I'm here."

"Where am I?"

"You're in the hospital. You're going to be okay."

"What happened?"

"Rest, Janene. We can talk more when you get settled in your room. We're headed there now."

The sound of Tom's voice soothed me, my partner. We could get through anything together. Men in light blue scrubs pulled me from the gurney to my hospital bed. It was then that I felt the weight hanging from my lower legs, two casts.

"You swerved off the road and crashed into the front window of Bruce's Hardware. The store wasn't open, and you missed hitting anyone on the sidewalk. You totaled your car. But, no one else was hurt."

I felt relieved that I didn't injure anyone else.

"X-rays revealed two broken tibias. The CT scan found no internal injuries. You're banged up and bruised, and more beautiful than the day I met you." Tom leaned in and brought my hand to his chest.

I shut my eyes and drifted off to sleep. Nurses with pain meds interrupted my slumber. A man in a white coat shined a penlight in my eyes. Another needle poked my arm. The blood pressure cuff squeeze woke me again. I just wanted to sleep.

I opened my eyes when I heard Hannah and Tom talking.

"That's a tough start to the new school year."

"She's going to bounce back," Tom said.

"Come here, sweetheart," I said, extending my arms to Hannah.

"I was so worried, Mom. What happened?"

"I'm not sure. The last thing I remember is my car accelerating toward a truck."

"The only thing that matters is that you're okay." Hannah reached for a tote bag that was sitting on the bedside dresser. "Here, I brought you an overnight bag. Do you want to put on comfy pajamas?"

"Yes, please. You know me well."

Dr. Frankle, a hospitalist who looked like an undergrad, came to my room two days later.

"Hello, Mrs. Branch. How are you feeling?"

"I've been better."

"We think you may have had a seizure, Do you have a history of seizures?"

"No."

"We've ruled out most everything else, and you appear to be healing well. Except for the injuries sustained in the car accident, you appear fine. I'll discharge you tomorrow."

I looked away, sending the message that I was done with the conversation. I fixed my gaze on the lemon yellow hospital wall and contemplated my throbbing and twitching legs.

"You'll go to Westbrook Rehab before going home. I'll arrange medical transport for tomorrow. You can go home when you are ambulatory with a walker."

The next morning, I heard a knock on my door.

"Mrs. Branch?"

"Come in."

Two young EMTs wearing navy blue uniforms walked into my room, rolling a gurney.

"Hello. Are you ready?"

"Yes. Please grab my bag from the dresser."

"Yes, ma'am."

They loaded me on their gurney and strapped me down.

"Geesh. Are you afraid I'm going to escape?"

"Hey! I know you, Mrs. Branch. Sorry, we don't want to drop you in the parking lot."

I glanced at his ID badge, Malcolm Bateman. I thought he looked familiar, a scruffy young man with an arduous past.

"Malcolm! Look at you."

"This is Mrs. Branch," Malcolm told his partner. "Best dang teacher I ever had."

"It's good to see you. You've done well for yourself."

"Yes, ma'am. You always believed I would make good."

"I knew there was something special about you."

Students like Malcolm brought me joy. Some students arrive at school, ready to learn. Others, like Malcolm, come to school seeking love and stability not found at home. I loved Malcolm even as he rejected my confidence. He began to trust me when he realized I wouldn't give up on him. I hoped he would see himself as I did, a capable young man who could succeed in spite of poverty and a history of self-destructive behavior.

Malcolm and his partner drove three blocks to my new home at the rehab center. I was grateful for the straps that held me on the gurney as we bounced along. They rolled me into the lobby. I'd never paid attention to ceilings before, a new perspective lying flat on my back with rows of fluorescent lights and ceiling tiles above me.

"Let's sit you up, Mrs. Branch."

Malcolm raised the gurney affording me a more comfortable view. His partner handed my paperwork to the receptionist, a slight woman behind the counter. She tucked her short, curly hair behind her ears and pushed up the middle of her glasses with an index finger before reaching for the envelope.

"Welcome to Westbrook Rehabilitation Center, Mrs. Branch. I'm Monica. I'll be helping you get checked in today."

Monica unfolded the paperwork and began typing on her keyboard. To my right, a stark, linoleum hallway carried the voice of an unhappy resident. Rows of ceiling lights substituted for daylight. I hoped my room had windows and that I only had to look through them for a day or two.

"Let's see. It looks like you're going to room 188. Right this way, please."

Malcolm and his partner followed Monica and rolled me to my room, and transferred me onto the bed.

"Take care, Mrs. B."

My room did have one window, covered with a closed miniblind.

Tom came to see me every day after work, and the kids visited when they could. At night, I counted ceiling tiles instead of sheep. Days turned into weeks. My bones healed, but my leg muscles wasted. My shins protruded, and my thigh and hip muscles twitched like worms racing below my skin. Why had my once-healthy body betrayed me? More tests. No answers.

I binged on TV shows and emailed lesson plans to unknown teachers who had been placed in charge of my classroom. I was largely ignored by the rehab staff save for Jessica. She entered my room with a cheerful smile, cracked the window blind, and cared for me like I was her mother.

"You are a rare bird, Miss Jessica. You are my sunshine, and my only sunshine in this place."

"Aw, thanks, Mrs. B. It's the least I can do for my favorite resident. Are you ready to start your day?"

Jessica rolled in a patient lift and gathered a sling from my bedside drawer.

"Let's get the bedding out of the way and get this party started." She stopped for a moment, held my hand, and looked into my eyes. "It's going to be a good day, Mrs. B."

I found solace in Jessica's compassion. She knew that I was a vulnerable human being and more than just a body to be moved. I felt safe and surrendered to her care. She bent my left knee, rolled my body to the right, and slipped the folded sling under me. Moving to the other side of the bed, she bent my right leg, rolled me to the left, and unfolded the sling underneath me.

"Lay back, and I'll get you ready to transfer."

Jessica attached four straps of the sling to the patient lift and raised me in the air like a hoist lifting an engine from a car.

"Are you ready to fly?"

I nodded yes, and the sling enveloped me like a venus flytrap catching its prey. Jessica rolled the lift and lowered me onto the bedside commode. She unhooked the sling and pushed the lift away.

"I'll give you some time to make the magic happen. Let me know when you're ready to shower," Jessica said as she handed me the call button.

I sat on the commode and prayed the laxatives would work this time.

Later that day, Dr. Frankle walked into my room, flipping through papers on his clipboard.

"Hello, Mrs. Branch. How are you feeling?"

"My legs don't hurt as much, but I'm not gaining strength, even with physical therapy. I'm beginning to doubt if I'm going to walk again."

"It's frustrating, I know. I wish I had an answer for you." He glanced at his clipboard again. "The lumbar puncture showed no signs of disease, specifically no MS, and I've run out of diagnostic tests. Is there something more I can do for you?"

"I'd like to keep searching for an answer."

"Yes, I would encourage you to do so. I can refer you to a neurologist."

"I'd rather go to my nurse practitioner first. She knows me well, and we can make a plan for what's next."

"That sounds like an excellent plan. Do you have family members at home who can help you with your daily activities?"

"Yes, my husband and teenage children."

"Since you have support, I can discharge you today if you feel ready to go home."

"I am totally ready to go home. That's the best news I've had all week."

"Sounds good. I'll write the discharge orders, and you can leave this afternoon. I wish you the very best, Mrs. Branch."

"Thank you."

I picked up my phone and texted Tom. "Going home today! Can you pick me up after work?"

Tom texted back, "Great news. I'll be there soon."

I leaned back in my hospital bed and smiled at the 63 ceiling tiles that I had counted nightly. I visualized the dark cloud leaving but feared it would follow me home.

CHAPTER TWO

Cora

Yarbrough Plantation
Near Westbrook, North Carolina
1863

Violence is the last refuge of the incompetent.
– Isaac Asimov

It started as an ordinary day in the quarters. Mama and I worked our chores together; Daddy and my little brothers, Samuel and Abner, tended the fields. Mama said that our family was lucky because we raised crops for use on the plantation. There was the Yarbrough family, livestock, and over two dozen Negros to feed. For that, a slave had to be trusted. Daddy planned and planted the cotton, corn, oats, and rye, and Mama grew and preserved vegetables and berries. It played an essential role on the plantation that carried a bit of respect too.

My daddy, Ernest, was born on the Yarbrough Plantation. His daddy raised crops for the plantation too. So, it was natural for my daddy to take over the job. My mama, Ada, wasn't so lucky. Master Yarbrough bought a lot of ten slaves at auction, but only needed eight. So Ada's mama and another woman were sold to a second buyer all those years ago. My mama was just a little girl.

"Cora, are you done shelling that basket of peas?" Ada said.

"Almost, Mama," I said.

"Set some aside before delivering them to the kitchen."

"Yes, Mama."

Today's work was all peas. I picked peas in the morning before the sun got too hot; I shelled peas in the afternoon in the cabin's shade. Mama boiled peas with salt and tried different ways to preserve them. This season she sealed jars of peas with beeswax. Daddy said Mama was the most clever woman in all the land. Yesterday was wild berry picking. I ate more berries than I put in my sack. Mama had no need to scold me because the stomach cramps last night were punishment enough. I finished shelling the basket of peas and left a bowl full on the table for Mama.

"I'm going to take the peas to the kitchen now."

I held the basket on my hip and made my way to the kitchen. I walked alongside the field and ran my fingers through the budding oats hoping to see Daddy along the way. The kitchen separated the main house from the fields and quarters. I was free to move about the plantation behind the kitchen but knew better than to be seen near the main house. I knocked on the wooden door of the mudbrick kitchen.

"Hello, Miss May? It's Cora. I've got a basket of peas."

"Come in, Cora. Put the basket on the table."

Miss May stood behind a table, kneading bread in a dusting of flour. Miss May was like an auntie to me. The story, as I've been told, was that Master Yarbrough didn't know or didn't care that he sold Ada's mama off without her. Ada came to Yarbrough Plantation, shackled in the back of a wagon with strangers. When the overseer unloaded the wagon, young Ada stood alone, clutching a homespun sack. Her mama handed her the sack seconds before they were torn apart and said,

"Ada, take this so you will remember me. Hold on tight and don't let go."

So young Ada stood in the yard alone with her sack, and Miss May took her straight away into her family and raised her as a little sister.

I placed the basket of peas on the table and breathed in the smell of fresh bread.

"Take the loaf on the end for your supper."

"Thank you, Miss May."

"Anything for you, sweet Cora. Now, be on your way."

I grabbed a loaf of fresh bread and made my way back home. Life on the Yarbrough Plantation had been quiet since the war began. Last week, Miss May told Mama that Master Yarbrough returned from battle, but his sons were still fighting. House gossip wasn't always the Lord's truth, but Mama Ada relished it the same. The latest was Mrs. Yarbrough could scarcely eat and was in a weakened state because she felt the winds of change coming.

There was no wind today, not even a breeze, as I walked past the fields on the way home. I looked across the way and saw Daddy with Samuel and Abner. I saw their britches and the bend of their backs as they pulled weeds from among the rye. I stopped to wave hello but ran behind a tree to hide when I saw three men walking toward Daddy. Mama told me to run and hide if I felt trouble brewing. I closed my eyes, hoping the men paid no mind to Daddy or my brothers.

I peeked around the tree at the moment a rifle butt came down on the back of Daddy's head. He fell to the ground. Samuel and Abner jumped on two of the attackers. Yet, they were too young to do more than distract them like bothersome flies. The round man peeled Samuel from his back and tossed him to the ground. I looked away, unable to watch anymore. I heard Abner cry out in horrible pain as I ran home.

"Mama! Mama!" I said, sounding more like an injured animal than a nine-year-old girl. "Daddy and the boys, three men in the field!"

"Calm down, child. I've no idea what you're saying."

"The men, they knocked Daddy to the ground. Sam and Abner too."

Two rifle shots sounded, then a third. Mama pulled me close, the loaf of bread still under my arm.

"Oh, Lord! No. We've got to run," Mama said as she grabbed my arm and her old homespun sack that hung on a hook by the door and headed outside.

A tall man was standing by the door and tripped Mama and me as we ran across the threshold and tumbled toward the ground. Mama crawled toward me, placed the sack behind me, and put herself between the devil who tripped us and me. I scooted my back toward the cabin wall. My heart pounded in my ears and screams stuck in my throat. The tall one, who looked to be a young Cherokee, glared down at us with his dark eyes. He grabbed the bread from under my arm and took a bite from the loaf. He kept it too.

The older, white one walked up to us and said, "Slow down Negros. You ain't goin' nowhere." Blood dripped from the knife blade brandished in Mama's face. The round, white man in a tattered grey jacket walked toward us and said, "Well, well. What do we have here?" His grimace exposed his rotten teeth as he scratched the stubble on his chin.

"We got two lady Negros here who need our attention," the old one said as sweat dripped off his greasy brow. The stench of the filthy men turned my stomach sour.

"Leave us alone," Ada muttered between clenched teeth.

"Oh, we got plans for you and your young one," the round one said.

The Cherokee grabbed Mama by her hair and yanked her to a standing position.

"Too bad Negro scalps ain't worth nothing."

The old one pushed Mama inside.

"I'll take the girl," the round one said.

"You a virgin or a little whore? I'm guessing you're a virgin, but you'll be a whore when I'm done with you."

I pressed against the cabin wall, not understanding his words but knowing they didn't bode well for me. I stayed silent and went numb as he pushed me into the dirt and made me a whore. He left me in a blood-smeared mess and went inside to look for food and valuables. The Cherokee followed him, and I found my

16

chance to escape.

I picked up Mama's sack and ran toward the quarters to find help and found the cabins empty. I ran into the woods and back toward the kitchen. I went inside and shut the door behind me.

"Miss May, help!" I leaned my back against the door and slid down to the floor. "Where are you, Miss May?" I bet she heard the gunshots and hid in the root cellar. I looked around the empty kitchen, wondering what to do and slid a loaf of bread into the sack.

"Forgive me Jesus for stealing this loaf of bread."

If the rogue soldiers were hungry, this would be their next stop. I opened the door just a crack to see if they were near and heard another gunshot.

"Mama!" I heard my mama in my mind say, Run, child. Run as fast as your feet can carry you.

I knew these fields and trees like the back of my hand. I'd spent hours picking wildflowers for my mama. I dreamed about being married to a man as handsome as my daddy and having children of my own -- a daughter to sing, sew, and laugh with me, and a son who would grow strong.

When our work was done, Sam, Abner, and I would fashion rifles out of twigs and play war around the hills. Of course, the Blue Coats won the war and set all the slaves free. The real war was in full swing, and we had our share of troops come through who laid claim to our food but never our bodies or lives.

I stopped behind the barn to catch my wind and see if the Confederates followed me. I didn't hear anything except the howling of a distant wolf and the snorting of a horse that knew something was amiss. I had to keep running before the devils tracked the scent of my fear. I squeezed the neck of Mama's sack and ran. I ran past the main house. It was once painted white, but weather and neglect left it looking like a flea-bitten gray mare. I didn't see anyone outside who would be concerned with me. But, my heart raced, I knew I was in trouble anyway. My family was gone. My life would never be the same.

I stopped when I sensed the end of the Yarbrough Plantation.

I knew too well the consequences of stepping outside the property; it was the point of no return. I'd be a runaway slave. Runaway or stay, either way, I'd be beaten or killed. Mama told me to run, so I ran. I came across a road and ran alongside it. I found a river and walked in the mud. I saw a meadow that led to the forest, so I traipsed through the lavender fields, not knowing where to go. I ran through the woods until the bottoms of my feet bled. The sun went down behind the mountains. I fell down under a tree, ate the stolen bread, and prayed that sleep would end my nightmare and bring me back to the comfort and safety of Daddy's arms.

CHAPTER THREE

Amadahy

Aguaquiri - indigenous land located in modern-
day Western North Carolina
200 years earlier, Planting Moon 1663

When the child is ill, the mother will know how to pray.
– Wasif Ali Wasif

My people of the Wolf Clan lived in Aguaquiri near the river with plentiful cane and fields of lavender. Mountains provided western territorial protection and homes for animals of beauty and sustenance. The river provided living water for fishing, drinking, and ceremonial cleansing. Women planted and tended the fields, and the Great Spirit blessed our village with bountiful harvests.

Cherokee tradition taught that all things are sacred and connected. The earth, sky, and living things worked in harmony to maintain balance. A balanced life respected all things in harmony. Balance, an elegant concept, eluded my spirit and my household.

I shared a home with my grandmother, mother, my husband Waya, and our twin girls. My grandmother, an honorable woman, received her due respect. My mother, a keeper of secrets, acted like an injured animal, striking first because she felt vulnerable. She trusted no one, and her insults pained me like hail during a summer storm.

I caught Waya's attention years ago during the crane dance when young women from the Wolf, Bear, and Long Hair Clans danced to attract a man from a neighboring tribe. That day, my grandmother handed me a basket of colorful feathers.

"Amadahy, take these to the village square and prepare for the crane dance."

"Grandmother, I don't want to participate in the crane dance with the other girls."

"You are no longer a girl. You're a woman now, and that is the reason you must. How else will you find a young hunter to court you?"

"I can hunt for myself."

"You will tend to crops and children. That is the custom of our ancestors," Grandmother said.

"That is enough nonsense, Amadahy. Take these feathers and prepare for the dance with the other women. It's time you found a husband," Mother said.

Not wanting to disobey my elders, I took the feathers and joined the other women. We decorated our dresses with feathers and practiced the slow, elegant dance we would perform for the young men. I couldn't understand the excitement shown by the other dancers. I felt more awkward than excited and hoped to blend in rather than be embarrassed. But after two nights of dancing around the sacred fire, Waya from the Long Hair Clan, noticed me.

The next day, Waya's aunt approached my mother and grandmother to seek permission for Waya to pursue me, and they gave their approval. Waya left the village to hunt for a worthy animal to present to me and returned the next day carrying a dressed buck over his shoulders. He left the offering at my door, hoping I would accept his gift and courtship. I sat inside, pondering this gift and the consequences of my acceptance.

"This Waya, he seems like an honorable man. He has completed his rite of passage and is an accomplished warrior and hunter. Amadahy, you should take this man into our family if he proves he can provide for you."

I hung my head in submission to my grandmother, unsure of my path.

"Amadahy, what are you waiting for? Do you think you are going to get another chance to find a husband? Go prepare the venison and invite Waya to join us for a meal."

"Yes, Mother."

I went out to prepare the food. I gathered onion and corn to complement the stew. Waya walked across the courtyard and sat to watch me cook. Mother and Grandmother joined him. This ritual assured Waya that I was ready to begin a courtship.

In the evenings, we joined other couples near the center of the lodge to talk and get to know each other under the watchful eyes of the elders. After a half-moon of our courtship, Waya walked me home.

"Let's go to the river and sit to see the rising moon and the stars overhead."

I walked with him, and we sat on a flat rock near the river. "Isn't it beautiful?" he said. "The stars are too many to count. I wonder what they are made of? I wish we could fly into the sky and become one with the stars."

I sat quietly, marveling at the sky above. Waya took my hand, leaning ever closer to me. I could feel his breath on my neck and smell his hair. I had no feeling of love for this man; but, it was time for me to begin a life as a married woman. Waya picked me up and laid me on the grass. I could hear the river rushing over the stones, singing to me as I ignored what was happening to my body. We rose from the ground, not speaking, and walked back to the village.

A moon later, Waya returned to the forest to hunt another deer. This time he brought the gift to my mother and grandmother to show that he could provide for me. They were happy to accept the offering of meat and invited Waya into our house for a meal. He stayed that night and became my husband. I felt a stirring in my womb, knowing a child had been conceived on the riverbank.

The child surprised us by being born two girls. Now, ten years later, our twins' sickbed covered the northwest corner of the house. Worn cane mats and a patchwork of pelts softened the dirt and straw floor. I sat between the girls, stroking their heads. Three days of fever left them tired and weak.

"Mama, I'm thirsty," Leotie said.

"Here, child."

I brought the last cup of water to her lips. Leotie lifted her head long enough for a sip. I tried to give Ahyoka a drink, but her neck fell limp against my arm. Instead, I dropped water from my fingers into her mouth.

Leotie and Ahyoka were identical in appearance, yet their spirits were as different as the east is from the west. Leotie, who appeared first, was like the owl and fox. She took her work seriously with her feet grounded in the soil. Ahyoka was like a young pup and rabbit from the east. She flowed like water. I could tell them apart by the hint of mischief in Ahyoka's eyes. I felt proud to be their mother. Together, they brought joy and balance to our family.

One season, when the girls were planting corn, Ahyoka asked Leotie to help her collect frogs instead. Leotie joined reluctantly as she knew the planting must be completed, or there would be nothing to harvest in the coming season. Ahyoka thought it helpful to give frogs to all the villagers to keep the insects away. So the girls gathered 30 frogs in a covered basket and released one frog into each home in the village. The crops were slow to be planted that year, but the villagers said they appreciated their gifts.

Another time, while I worked in the fields, Ahyoka convinced Leotie to sneak down to the river to play. They swam like a fish even at an early age, but they were too young to be at the river alone. They busied themselves by building a dam of rocks. Leotie stayed on the shore gathering rocks while Ahyoka dove into the river and placed one stone at a time. She swam to the point of exhaustion, lost her footing, and the current swept her downriver. Leotie dove in after her and met the same fate. The village people searched day and night. At sunrise, a young man found them sleeping on the river bank and brought them home. Escaping death convinced Leotie to rein in Ahyoka's antics. Now, they stared at death again.

Waya opened the blanket that hung over the door, and daylight flooded the room.

"It smells like death in here," he said as he hung the woven blanket over antler hooks on the door and walked inside.

"Your criticism is not helpful."

"How can I be helpful, Amadahy?"

"Take these bowls to the river and bring back some living water."

He picked up the bowls and headed to the river without saying a word. I'd been seeking out the imbalance causing my girls' illness. Waya admitted that he forgot to honor the life of a buck he killed two months ago. He dishonored its sacrifice, and by doing so, he dishonored our household. Waya refused to remedy his mistake when I pointed out the error. He had distanced himself from me; while this was not unusual, he no longer paid attention to the fate of our girls. It wasn't surprising that at least one evil spirit found an opening and brought illness into my family. I felt the weight of shame for allowing this to happen. I prayed and focused on restoring balance to our family.

I opened my medicine bag and emptied the contents. I held the white rabbit foot to my cheek and thanked the rabbit's spirit for providing nourishment and spiritual balance. I turned my attention to the sacred stones and tumbled them in my hands. I prayed to the healing powers of the stones as I placed them to the north, south, east, and west. I filled in the remainder of the circle with stones of color while I acknowledged the seasons in the circle of life.

Tears of grief and gratitude rolled down my cheeks as I prayed,

"Grandfather to the east,

I am grateful for your wisdom.

23

Grandmother to the east,
I am grateful for your wisdom.
Oh, Great Spirit,
your warm winds restore balance and bring healing.
Oh, Great Spirit,
  bring healing to my children."

I opened my eyes to find a white rabbit seated in my stone circle. It wiggled its nose at me and sniffed the eastern stones before darting outdoors.

Leotie cried out, "Etsi, Etsi."

"Mother is here."

Leotie struggled to sit up, but she didn't have the strength.

"Be still."

"I had a terrible vision in my dream," Leotie said.

"Tell me about it."

"It was so disturbing, I cannot give it power by speaking it aloud."

I returned the prayer stones to my medicine bag and brought the rabbit foot to Leotie's cheek.

"Your thoughts are pure, and your words hold power. I'm here to listen when you are ready to tell your story."

Leotie reached her arm out and turned her head toward Ahyoka.

"Sister, are you there? Don't leave me."

"Ahyoka is here, but the fever has taken her strength."

"Mother, please move me closer to her. I need to be next to her."

I picked up Leotie and laid her next to her sister. Leotie placed her arm on Ahyoka and returned to sleep. My heavy spirit lifted at the precious gesture, and gratitude settled in my bones. I stepped outside to clear my head as Waya returned with water.

"Thank you. Leave the water inside."

I inhaled the fresh air and anticipated another difficult conversation.

"What is it, Waya? Why are our girls suffering?"

We have caused an imbalance, obviously, Amadahy."

"What do you suppose it to be?"

The sun moved further to the west as we sat together in silence. I feared that Waya would leave me, although I hoped that he would. My own father was a mystery, and my mother never taught me about the complexities of marriage. I tried to respect my husband.

The setting sun caught Waya's hair as he stood up and walked away. He returned a while later mounted on his horse. He tossed a dead, white rabbit at my feet, nodded and rode south, leaving a ni wa ya, the Wolf Clan and returning to a ni gi lo hi, the Long Hair Clan.

CHAPTER FOUR

Janene

Westbrook, North Carolina
2013

In the social jungle of human existence,
there is no feeling of being alive without a sense of identity.
– Erik Erikson

I was scheduled to go back to work the week after Thanksgiving break. The problem was, Westbrook High School was built in 1929 and had no elevator to take me to the second floor. Nick Campbell, the new math teacher, had agreed to swap classrooms with me. Tom and Daniel spent the weekend packing up and moving 24 years of teaching to my new home in room 113.

"Nick, I can't thank you enough for switching with me."

"No problem. You're a Wolf Pack legend around here. I'm happy to do anything I can to make your job easier. And on a selfish note, it'll be easier to get my 10,000 steps going up and down those stairs all day."

I rolled my wheelchair into my new classroom and surveyed the sterile walls. I loved my job. I loved my school. I loved my students. What was my life if I didn't have my Wolf Pack? I'd spent my entire career here, poured my heart and soul into this place. I was nothing without it. I had to figure out what was going on so I could return to my love at Westbrook High with my body and mind intact.

"Thanks, guys. It's been a tough day. Don't know what I'd do without you."

Daniel grunted without looking up from his omnipresent phone. It was uncharacteristic of him to not engage. Maybe it was hormones leading him into manhood and away from his mother. When we got home, I went straight to bed. Sleep came quickly, and I dreamed of running.

I awoke the next day to Tom tracing his fingers down my spine.

"Good morning, sexy," Tom whispered in his Barry White voice.

I rolled onto my back and combed my fingers through my hair.

"Seriously? I'm a hot mess. Not feeling so sexy these days," I said, pushing Tom away.

My words and actions betrayed my feelings. I longed to be desired and ached for Tom's attention. While on my back, he took the opportunity to explore my breasts. His pleasure was making itself known against my thigh. It was a great way to start the day.

Hannah drove Daniel and me to school the morning I returned to work. My car retraced the route taken months ago on the day of my accident. I winced as we passed Bruce's Hardware and I saw my reflection in the new storefront windows. My wheelchair and emotional trauma were the only remnants of that day. We drove onto campus greeted by trees with red and golden leaves. Hannah pulled into the first accessible parking spot and placed the temporary placard on the rearview mirror of my new Camry. She popped open the trunk and hopped out of the driver's seat, waving goodbye to Daniel.

"Thanks for the help, jerk!"

She hoisted my wheelchair from the trunk and pushed the arms of the chair down to open it. She rolled the chair next to me and lifted my arms to extract me from the front seat. I steadied myself on the door well and shifted my weight from the car and into the chair. I glanced around to see who was staring at the freak show. It was early, so no one was there to witness my struggle. Hannah hung our backpacks on the back of the wheelchair, handed me my coffee, and rolled me to my new home in classroom 113. Bending down, she put her hand on my shoulder and gave me a quick kiss on the cheek.

"Welcome back, Mom. Your students will be glad to see you rather than a revolving door of substitute teachers."

"Thanks, honey." I placed my hand on hers. "I'm glad to be back."

My classroom looked presentable, thanks to the efforts of my two favorite men. Desks were moved closer to the far wall giving me room to get around in my wheelchair. I rolled up to my desk and turned on my laptop. Three hundred and seventy-five unread email messages greeted me.

"Ugh, those can wait," I said out loud and snapped the laptop shut.

I rolled over to the bookshelf and dropped peppermint and orange essential oils into the apple-shaped diffuser. Tom thoughtfully left everything I needed on the lower shelves. I inhaled and tried to shake the black cloud, but it refused to leave. Kids trickled into the classroom and greeted me with excitement and hugs. Their joy temporarily broke through my darkness like unexpected rays of sun on a cloudy day.

I made it through my first day back though I could barely keep my eyes open or hold my head upright. Hannah met me in my room after school.

"Hi, honey! How was your day?"

"Good. My AP Calculus class is killing me."

"You'll have to ask your dad for help with that."

Tom was an electrical engineer for Trident Technologies, he designed communication systems for the U.S. Army. His company was based in Asheville, and he was fortunate enough to work from home except for occasional trips to Fort Bragg or the

Pentagon. His work was classified, and he rarely spoke of it. That fit Tom's personality well, intelligent and kind, yet intensely private. He helped the kids with math and science. I was more adept with English and the social sciences.

"Let me know if you need help with your senior essay. I can handle that."

"I've got your brains, Mom. Dad's mechanical mind, not so much. How did it feel to be back in your classroom?"

"It felt good to be back with my kids. But for the love of all things holy, I can't keep my eyes open. Can you pick up Daniel from weight training?"

"I've got a study date with Bryant this afternoon. He seems to have this math thing figured out and can't wait to share it with me."

"Okay, maybe Dad can pick him up. I'm passing out the minute I get home."

Hannah rolled me into my bedroom. I slid onto the toilet to pee with the grace of an elephant. I sat there for a minute, wondering why was my body failing me.

I texted Tom, "Can you pick up Daniel from school at 6:00?" I put the phone in my lap and cradled my hands over my face. I wiped my nose and took a deep breath. I pulled myself off the toilet and sat in my wheelchair, air swished from out of the seat cushion. I rolled next to my bed and used every ounce of remaining energy to transfer. Sleep came as my head touched the pillow.

Saturday morning, Hannah and I planned our girl's day over oatmeal and bananas. Hannah tells me, "Steel-cut oats are good for your heart."

"You're good for my heart," I said. "What are we doing today?"

"How about pedicures?"

"Perfect. Would you mind if Lisa and Kelsey joined us? I

haven't seen Lisa since her surgery."

"Sure. I'll text Kelsey and see if they can come."

Lisa and I met when she moved to the neighborhood 15 years ago. Hannah and Kelsey were in preschool together, and the four of us had been friends since. Lisa had breast cancer; I had my own health issues and hadn't been there for her. I was glad to have a chance to catch up.

"We are set for 11:00 at Nail Envy," Hannah said.

"Can't wait. Would you mind helping me get ready?"

Hannah and I enjoyed our morning together. I noticed she seemed worried and had spent more time with me than in her previous teen years. I wished I knew what to tell her.

"Let's go. Or, should I say let's roll?" Hannah said as she pushed my wheelchair to the car. We drove to the nail salon, and with the aid of a parking fairy, found an open, accessible parking spot near the shop.

"How lucky is that?"

"Let's head inside, I see Lisa and Kelsey waiting."

Hannah got my wheelchair from the trunk and transferred me from the front seat. We entered the salon, greeted by hugs and the joy of friendship.

"Let's be The Pink Ladies," Kelsey said with four shades of pink nail polish in her hands.

"I'll take this one," Hannah said as she and Kelsey walked to their chairs, and Lisa and I followed.

"It's been too long," I said to Lisa contemplating her appearance.

"It's been a rough few months."

Lisa's stylish scarf didn't hide chemotherapy's toll. She looked at me with brown eyes that outshone her dappled, gray face.

"What's been going on?" I asked.

"I'm done with chemo for now. Recovering from surgery has been harder than I'd expected."

A coughing fit interrupted her, and I shuffled through my purse to find a tissue. She took a deep breath and wiped her mouth.

"I'm sorry you're going through this; I can't imagine."

"It's no picnic. But, I'm hopeful this time. What about you? A wheelchair?"

"Strange, I know. The doctors can't figure out what's wrong. It's disheartening, as you know."

"Are you going to sit in the pedicure chair?" Sandy, the nail technician, asked, pointing to the row of chairs. I had followed Sandy to three different salons over the years. Not only was she excellent at her job, but I had also grown to love her. She came to see me while I was recovering at the rehab center and kept my manicure looking good.

"No, thanks, Sandy. I'll stay in my chair," I said, disappointed I'd miss a relaxing foot soak. I looked around the salon, noting the mirrors and collages of earth tones. The waterfall trickling over stones reminded me of walks by the river. The pungent assault of acetone and acrylic compounds contradicted the serene ambiance.

I turned to Lisa. "How are you able to process all of this without losing your mind?"

"I don't know if I'm handling it well, sometimes I just lose it. Pain is awful, but the worst part is not having the energy to do the things I want to do. It's like I run out of gas after a trip around the block."

"I can relate to that."

"I try to take it a day at a time," Lisa said.

"I should try that; worrying about tomorrow is not serving me well."

I handed Sandy the Perpetually Pink nail polish, and she began scrubbing my toenails with cotton and polish remover.

"Your feet are in good shape, Janene. This won't take long at all."

"No heel calluses, an upside of not being able to walk," I said.

"Every cloud has a silver lining."

I leaned back and thought about the positive things and people in my life, Tom, my kids, a job that gave me purpose. I closed my eyes and pictured myself running in a lavender field, sunshine on my face. I saw my mom's coiffed, brown hair and petite frame as we built sandcastles on the beach. I felt her warmth and caught a hint of her hairspray. I looked up to see her face, but the sun obscured my view. I squinted in an attempt to see her one last time, silently pleading with the universe to not let me forget. How could I forget my mother's face? Her warmth left me as my mind drifted further. My legs grow weaker, Daniel hates me, Tom is bored with me, I can't work. People yell at me to get out of the way. I'm shrinking. I'm invisible. My thoughts controlled me on an endless loop.

"Janene."

I opened my eyes and saw Lisa kneeling next to me.

"Look at me, Janene. I'm here. You're safe."

I made eye contact as Lisa reached for my hands.

"Name five things you can see."

"I see you, the sink, rows of nail polish, Hannah, and the lady in the green jacket."

"Good. Now, tell me three things you can feel." Lisa looked at Sandy and made a drinking motion. Sandy nodded and walked to the back of the salon.

"I can feel my wheelchair, your hand, and my jeans."

"Excellent. Take a deep breath. You're here with us."

I drank the water Sandy offered.

"My mind races, and my thoughts take off like crazy."

"You're not crazy. You've got a lot going on, and you're just trying to make sense of it all," Lisa said. "It's happened to me too."

"You seem calm like you have it all together. How do you manage?"

"Therapy has helped. I'm learning to stop and redirect negative thoughts before I get to the point of freaking out." Lisa returned to her pedicure seat, and Sandy moved her stool next to me.

"Sorry about that, Sandy."

"Don't worry. I just want you to be okay. Now, let me finish your Perpetually Pink toes."

We finished without talking, giving me some time to recover. I overheard the lady in the green jacket talking to her friend.

"You know Claire? She had a complete breakdown. Just between you and me, I heard she took a whole bottle of pills. She even left a note that said she was tired of the pain and wanted it to be over. Such a shame."

Lisa looked at me and rolled her eyes, referring to the tactless oversharing by the lady in the green jacket. I nodded my head in agreement.

The four of us sat at the dryer table comparing our pink toes.

"We better stay for a few extra cycles to be sure our toes are dry enough for socks and shoes," Hannah said.

"Who's up for going to the riverwalk when we're done here?" Kelsey asked. "I'd like to go shopping."

"Sounds good to me. I need some new shoes," Hannah said.

"What do you think?" Lisa said, looking at me.

"Let's grab a bite while the girls shop. I've got a few questions if you don't mind."

I embraced the idea of some fresh air at the riverwalk. The crisp air bit the tip of my nose as we neared the river. Leaves crunched under my wheels in an unfamiliar pattern.

"We're heading to the stores, Mom. Should we meet back here at two?"

"Perfect," Lisa said.

Hannah touched my shoulder on her way. Lisa and I watched the girls walk, their long hair waving back.

"Look at those two young beauties," Lisa said, "Such grace and confidence. By looking at them, you'd never know their mamas are such a mess."

We found a table inside and ordered hot tea and butter cookies to share.

"Thanks for helping me in the salon. How did you know I was freaking out on the inside?"

"You looked okay like you were relaxing. But, I grew concerned when you wouldn't answer me," Lisa said.

"It was helpful to name what I could see and feel."

"It's grounding, right? That is something my therapist asked me to try."

"My thoughts and emotions get the best of me."

"Is that helpful? It only makes the situation worse for me."

I sat back and searched for an answer. My emotions naturally prevailed.

"Not at all. But, how do you stop it? I don't think about it, only react."

"Thinking about it is the first step. When negative thoughts start bouncing in my head, I pause and ask, 'Is this true? Is this helpful?' If not, and it's usually a big, fat lie, I dismiss the thought and replace it with something I know to be true."

"Sure, that makes perfect sense. But, how on earth do you control your mind and emotions like that?"

"I learned about mindful meditation at my support group. It starts with being aware of yourself physically, mentally, and emotionally. Check-in with yourself and acknowledge what's going on. Don't judge yourself. Don't we do that enough?"

"Absolutely," I said. "I'm a mess physically, mentally, and emotionally. Check!"

"Funny. But seriously, this exercise helps uncover what is preventing me from being present in the moment."

"I believe it certainly works for you. Me? I don't know. I'm not really into that kind of stuff."

"No worries. Find what works for you," Lisa said.

"I'm angry and depressed. I guess it's fear of not knowing what is happening to me. I'm afraid that soon I won't be able to work anymore; I just don't have the energy to get through the day. Who am I without my Wolf Pack? It's all I've ever known."

"You're so much more than your job, Janene. You need to find your real identity. Deepak Chopra says, 'We have to really educate ourselves in a way about who we are, what our real identity is.'"

"I'm just me, Janene Branch, History teacher, and Queen of

the Wolf Pack."

"That's your job, not the essence of who you are."

"How do you find happiness without your veterinary practice? Hasn't that been your dream your whole life? And, all that school, all those years? Don't you feel like it's been ripped away from you?"

"Sure, I miss it. But, my partner has the practice under control. I'm hoping it's just a temporary thing, and I will be able to go back to work. But if," Lisa hesitated. "But if I'm terminal, I don't want to be miserable for the time I have left on this earth."

"You're amazing, Lisa. I'm stuck in 'depressed and afraid.' I can't shake it."

"Keep searching, Janene. You'll find your answer."

I went to see my nurse practitioner the following week. Laura had been my primary care doctor since Daniel was born. She had taken the time to listen, gave me her best advice, and ultimately let me manage my own health. But, this time was different. I didn't know what to do. Laura walked into the exam room and couldn't hide her surprise when she saw me in a wheelchair.

"Janene! Good to see you. What brings you in today?"

"Hi, Laura. I'm not able to walk."

"I see that."

"I'm also experiencing unbelievable fatigue." My throat stopped me as I broke into sobs. "I don't think I can continue working." My voice trailed off an octave higher than it started. "I've no idea what's happening to my body. I feel like normalcy and stability are out of my reach."

Laura nodded.

"I have this dark cloud looming over me, and I can't shake it."

"How can I support you through this, Janene?"

"I'm at a loss. I've no idea."

"I've looked through all the tests Dr. Frankle did in the hospital, and I can't find anything he missed. What have you found on the Internet?"

"You know me too well. Of course, I've been Googling for months. But seriously, the only thing I can find is something neurological."

"It's a possibility, unfortunately. But I can't be sure. Let me refer you to a neurologist at Duke who specializes in motor neuron disease. I can prescribe an antidepressant as well," Laura said.

"Okay."

"What about work? I think you should take a leave of absence until we can figure out what's going on. All this stress can't be helping."

"I love my job and hate the thought of leaving. It's who I am. My classroom is the only place I feel alive."

"What about fatigue, do you have the energy to make it through the day?"

"No. It's hard. I guess I have to stop until we figure out what's going on."

"Okay. I'll send the paperwork to the school district office and make a referral to neurology."

Laura gave my shoulder a sympathetic squeeze as she left the exam room. "I'm sorry, Janene."

I thought about what Lisa said about finding my identity. What is my true identity? If I'm not Mrs. Branch, Queen of the Wolfpack, then who am I?

CHAPTER FIVE

Cora

Westbrook, North Carolina
1863

There is a reason it used to be a crime in the Confederate
states to teach a slave to read: Literacy is power.
– Matt Taibbi

I heard the sound of boys talking and felt the warmth of the
morning sun on my face. A gentle nudge of my shoulder
woke me halfway.

"You okay? Hey. Wake up."

It took me a minute to understand what was happening. I
squinted against the sun and stared at the two boys bending
over me. I thanked Jesus that they were Negro boys.

"It's okay. We're not going to hurt you. What's your name?"

I scooted myself to a seated position against the tree that
was my shelter the night before. The horror of yesterday's
events resurfaced when I saw my torn and bloodied dress. It felt
as though my body didn't belong to me. I reached for the comfort of my necklace.

"Now, now. Don't be afraid. My name is Eli, and this is my
brother, Lewis. What's your name?"

I stared straight ahead.

"Maybe she's deaf or something," Lewis said.

"Can you hear me? We want to help you," Eli said.

I responded to their kindness with silence.

"I don't think I've seen you around these parts before," Lewis said.

Eli reached out his hand.

"Here, let me help you up."

The boys took hold of my arms and stood me up. I was numb to the pain as my torn up feet bore my weight.

"Come with us. We will take you to our mama, Miss Hattie," Eli said. "She will know what to do."

"Do you know Miss Hattie?" Lewis asked. "She helps all the colored children in town. She can help find your family or teach you to read. Would you like that?"

"I don't think she understands what we are saying," Eli said.

My feet shuffled in the dirt as if shackled in leg irons. Eli and Lewis coaxed me along like I was a kitten caught under the porch.

"You must be thirsty, Miss. Just a little longer and we will be home. What should we call you?" Eli said.

"I'm thirsty and hungry," Lewis said.

"You're always hungry, dear brother."

We walked alongside a dirt road and came upon the edge of town. I looked up from the ground and saw the people greeting one another and conducting business. Colored people walked among others like they were free. I'd only been to town once before with Mama. It was springtime. Mrs. Yarbrough ordered a fancy dress from a free Negro woman who sewed dresses for the finest women in Washington DC. Rumors went around saying it was the same seamstress who sewed for the First Lady herself. I'm not sure why the Misses would need such a dress, but anyway, I walked to town with Mama to pick up the dress. That's the only time I had any business in Westbrook.

We walked up to a mud and stone house standing at the end of the main street. It was hard to believe that colored people lived in a house that big. My nose recognized the sizzling pork fat as we got closer to the back door. The smell comforted me as it reminded me of Mama's kitchen. Yet, my stomach rejected the thought of food.

"Mama, we've got company," Lewis said as we walked into the kitchen from the back door.

"Company? I love company," Hattie said. "Come in, come in."

Hattie smiled at me with her gapped-tooth grin. Hattie must have been a queen from the old country. Mama told me queens had a gap in the middle of their teeth. Flour dusted the beautiful coffee skin on her arms as she carried a raw biscuit in her hand.

"We're just in time for some breakfast. Ask anybody. Miss Hattie's breakfasts are the best you'll ever find," Lewis said as he patted his belly.

"Who is this lovely young lady?" Hattie asked as she put the biscuit dough on the counter and guided me to sit on a kitchen stool.

"We don't know, Mama," Eli said. "We found her asleep under a tree as we were walking home from the William's place. She doesn't talk. It's like she's seen a ghost."

"Give her some time, let's give her some time," Hattie said.

I sat silently on the kitchen stool and stared at the ground as the household whirled around me. I'd never been with strangers in a strange place. Yet somehow, I felt safe with Miss Hattie. Hattie made me a plate, and it remained untouched on the counter.

"Mama, we are going down to the mill. Mr. Morgan's got some work for us," Eli said. "Anything you need before we go?"

"No, son, I'll be spending time with our new girl, and I've got the Rippy kids coming over this afternoon. Make me proud, you two."

"Yes, ma'am. We'll be home by sundown."

Lewis picked up the sack of hardtack and jerky Hattie had packed for their lunch. He stuffed an extra helping in the bag outside of Hattie's watchful eye.

"You eat more than a horse, young man," Hattie said as she left the kitchen.

"I swear that woman has eyes on the back of her head," Lewis said as he followed Eli out the back door.

Hattie came back into the kitchen, carrying a blue wrapper that looked practically new. She spread it out on the table and pressed the fabric with the palms of her hands. Next, she prepared a basin with hot water and set a cloth and soap on the counter.

"Here we go dear; Let's get you cleaned up a bit. I've got some fresh soap and a clean dress." She pulled up a kitchen stool next to me and picked up my hands and held them. "Sweet girl. You've had a rough time. What should I call you, dear one?"

I felt my lips tremble and my head shake the slightest bit back and forth. My lips parted, and a squeak escaped my dry throat.

"It's going to be alright. Mama Hattie is here."

Hattie dipped the cloth in the warm water and rubbed it with soap. She ever so gently drew the rag up my arms. I relented to her touch as she continued and removed my blood-stained dress. Hattie hummed a familiar tune as she rhythmically washed me from my ears to my toes. I heard Mama sing the song in my head.

The Gospel train's comin'
I hear it just at hand
I hear the car wheel rumblin'
And rollin' thro' the land
Get on board little children
Get on board little children
Get on board little children
There's room for many more

She draped the clean wrapper over my head as her song came to an end.

"There we go. The wrapper is a little big, but you will certainly grow. You must be feeling better. Now let's have a look at your hair."

Hattie unwrapped the rag from my head, exposing the cornrows my mama braided last Sunday.

"Oh my! These are beautiful braids, dear one. Did your mama

do this?"

I looked into Hattie's eyes for the first time and tried to express my gratitude. My words were buried somewhere deep.

"It's okay, dear one. It's going to be okay." Hattie wrapped my hair in a clean, green cloth with small, yellow flowers. Her arms drew me close to her bosom.

I should not be alive, yet I found comfort in the arms of a stranger. I was a runaway slave and a little whore. I did not deserve such kindness. I was a coward who ran to save myself and left my family for dead. I should be dead alongside them.

"Now, dear one, the Rippy children are coming over to work on their reading, then we will have supper to prepare. I could use your help."

I followed Hattie into the front room. The house had separate rooms, like two cabins built together. There were two places for fire, one in the kitchen and one in the gathering room. This room had a long table with benches and a rocking chair by the empty fire stones. The rocking chair looked like the one Daddy had. He would sit for a spell in the evening before turning in for the night.

"Have a seat at the table. The children will be here shortly."

Hattie opened a door that led to another room with a bed and sleeping pallets. She disappeared into the room and came out carrying a small box and placed it in the middle of the table.

"This here is a slate, and this is chalk," Hattie said. She picked up the small white piece and looked at it. "This was a recent gift from the grandfather of one of my students. Give it a try. You can write on the slate with the chalk. We used to write our letters with a stick in the dirt. This is a better way."

Hattie put the chalk to the slate, drew three lines, and handed it to me.

"This is the letter A. I can teach you to read and write, dear one. Would you like that?"

I picked up the chalk and rubbed the tips of my fingers together and noticed it looked like flour. A knock at the door startled me, and I pushed the slate and chalk toward the center of the table. Hattie opened the door to the outside, and three children walked in and sat down at the table.

"Good afternoon, children," Hattie said.

"Good afternoon, Miss Hattie," the children said in unison. A girl who looked to be about my size greeted me with a smile.

"Hi. My name is Meriday. These are my little brothers, Oscar and Lil' John."

I acknowledged Meriday with a slight nod.

"Let's get busy, children. We will begin with a review of the alphabet. Oscar, please begin."

Oscar stood up with his arms straight at his side and his chest puffed out, and said, "A B C D E F G, H I J K L M N O P, Q R S, T U V, W X Y, and Z" He finished with a grin.

"Well done. Yes, sir," Hattie said.

"Meriday, can you read the first passage in the Book of Saint John?"

Hattie handed her an open Bible. I looked around and listened to hear if anyone outside would be able to hear Meriday reading. Miss May told Mama that one day, a house slave was found to have a Bible, and he was whipped near to death. He had to leave the house and became a field hand. Master Yarbrough said a Negro with a book could not be trusted in the house. I hoped Meriday would not meet the same fate.

Meriday placed the Bible in front of her and moved her finger over it as she read.

"In the beginning was the Word, and the Word was with God, and the Word was God."

Meriday read slower than she talked, but she was still good at it.

"Keep going," Hattie said.

"The same was in the beginning with God. All things were made by him; and without him was not any thing made that was made. In him was life; and the life was the light of men. And the light shineth in darkness; and the darkness comprehended it not."

"Good. Now can you tell me what that means?"

"I'm afraid not, Miss Hattie." Meriday looked down.

"Chin up, now. We are here to learn. Jesus is from God, and Jesus is God. Jesus came to be our light. But, we don't always understand it."

"Yes, ma'am," Meriday said.

"We all can learn."

Everything I knew, I learned from my mama. I could learn from Miss Hattie too. I watched the rest of the lessons, wondering what it would be like to read and write. I would have taught Samuel and Abner to read and write. Daddy would've beamed with pride.

The children left when their lessons were done, and Hattie turned her attention to supper in the kitchen. Hattie opened the pot and inhaled. The ham hock and beans had been simmering all day.

"Oh, Lordy. That smells mighty good. Do you know how to bake up some cornbread, dear one?"

I'd been making cornbread since I was knee-high to my mama. I searched the larder for cornmeal, flour, baking soda, and lard. Slim chance of finding the sugar. Hattie returned from the yard with eggs and fresh milk and put them on the table.

"Here, you'll need these," Hattie said as she set down a bowl and sifter. "Looks like you've got everything but sugar."

Hattie bent down and retrieved a tin canister from a low cabinet and raised it with both hands.

"Here we have the sugar. I have to hide it from Lewis."

I got busy making the cornbread. It was a nice distraction, doing something worthwhile. Hattie sat on a kitchen stool and rested with a cup of water.

"Look at you, precious one. You do know your way around the kitchen. You've been well cared for, not like some children who happen at my door. More times than not, they haven't seen a washtub in months, and they have swollen bellies from hunger."

Hattie left the kitchen and returned with a basket of darning and set it on the table. She picked up a gray sock and pulled it over her hand, looking for holes.

"My boys are sure hard on their socks, but I caught this one in time. I'll fix this right up."

I set the cornbread skillet over the fire and joined Hattie at the table. I looked at her and reached for the sock and thread.

"You sew too?"

Hattie handed me the sock and a threaded needle, and I set to work. Hattie picked a sock to darn herself.

"Like I was saying, you're a special young lady. You are well cared for and loved. Your mama taught you well. I surely hope we can find her."

I handed Hattie the mended sock, and she gave me a pair of britches.

"That seam needs sewing, there," She said, pointing to the back end. "Now, most children find their way to me after their parents have passed or the children get lost or left behind. They are hungry and afraid, so I love and nurse them back to health. I scrub them clean and find them a free family. Never in my life would I turn a child over to be owned by another. I would rather send one underground. Believe me."

Eli and Lewis returned from their day's work at Morgan's Mill smelling of sawdust and sweat. It was a different smell than my daddy's when he returned from the day's work in the field. Sawdust had a hint of sweet and the field smelled of something grown from the earth.

"I'm famished. Something smells straight from Heaven," Lewis said.

"We made your favorite supper," Hattie said.

"I am ready," Eli said.

"Go wash for supper, Y'all smell like a hard day's work."

The boys did as Hattie asked, and we sat down to eat.

"Give thanks, Eli, before we eat," Hattie said.

"Dear Lord, we thank ye for this supper. Bless the hands that prepared it. Thank ye for the roof over our head and the love in our home. Amen."

"Amen," Hattie and Lewis said.

Eli and Lewis dove into the beans and cornbread. Hattie made me a bowl and placed it in front of me, but I couldn't muster the courage to eat.

"How was your day at the mill?" Hattie asked.

"We had a good day, Mama," Eli said. "Unloaded a boatload of logs and loaded it up again with fresh-cut lumber."

"Mr. Morgan said we were hard workers and gave us these," Lewis said as he placed two silver coins on the table.

"Well done, boys," Hattie said. "Well done. Two quarters, that's fifty cents in all -- we will eat well for the rest of the month. Hattie's grin revealed her relief.

"Did you hear about what happened at the Yarbrough Plantation yesterday?" Eli asked.

My heart dropped to the pit of my stomach. I made myself small like Mama did when the Yarbrough sons came to give attention she didn't ask for.

"Do tell, son," Hattie said.

"They're saying a slave family got attacked and killed, probably by a crew from Thomas' army. They found a man, woman, and two boys. Supposed to be a girl too, but they didn't find her body," Lewis said.

Three pairs of eyes turned to me at once, mouths opened, cornbread crumbs fell to the table. I picked up my spoon and ate my supper.

CHAPTER SIX

Amadahy

Aguaquiri
Green Corn Moon, 1663

We don't heal in isolation but in community.
– S. Kelley Harrell

G awonii, the medicine man, returned from a week in the rock caves with the Dogwood Little People. His meetings there were sacred and secret, and the old men say the Little People were a race of spirits reaching two feet tall with hair like a horse mane. These handsome and mysterious people loved music and dance. Some say you could hear the song of their drums, but you must not follow their song as they do not like to be disturbed by strangers. Gawonii, whose name means he who is speaking, is one of many generations of Cherokee healers who have visited the Little People once a year to dance to the green corn moon and share healing remedies.

I approached Gawonii midday as he tended to his larder, seeking healing for my daughters.

"Di-da-nv-wi-s-gi, welcome back. I come to you with an urgent matter."

"Greetings, Amadahy. How may I help you today?"

"My daughters are very ill and need healing."

"Of course, Amadahy. Let me get my medicine bag, and we will be on our way."

Gawonii listened as we walked.

"My girls have suffered from fever for many days. Leotie is alert but weak; Ahyoka goes in and out of consciousness."

"Have you given thought to the root of the imbalance in your home?"

"Yes. I'm afraid Waya and I are to blame. I believe Waya has been killing animals without expressing gratitude, and our marriage is over. Waya returned to his clan."

"That leaves room for an evil spirit to enter your home and cause suffering," Gawonii said.

"I'm ashamed."

"There's hope, Amadahy. Let's restore balance and see if health will return."

My mother and grandmother tended to the girls as Gawonii smudged the house with white sage and cedar. He chanted prayers of his forefathers as smoke purified the air.

"Oh, Great Spirit, whose voice I hear in the winds, and whose breath gives life to all the world, hear my cry. Grandfather to the east, Grandfather to the south, Grandfather to the west, Grandfather to the north, hear my cry. Restore balance to this dwelling. Bring healing to all who dwell here. I ask for specific healing to be brought forth to Leotie and Ahyoka. Restore their health and the vibrancy of their youth. I offer white sage to remove the negative energy and spirit. I offer sweetgrass to attract positive energy and balance."

Gawonii waved the burning offering in an infinity loop throughout the lodge. His face didn't hide his annoyance of having all of us in the house.

"I'm sensing a profusion of negatively. It's more than a single spirit. I sense condemnation that is keeping this household in sickness."

Gawonii brought the burning sage to each adult to cleanse our auras from pain and judgment. I looked at my mother, and our eyes met, and I felt inadequate. She acted surprised that I could reap a crop because I behaved more like a boy who hunted than a girl who tended fields. I've tried to be an honorable daughter, yet I've made mistakes and have disappointed her. I made a significant mistake allowing Waya to have his way with me on the riverbank all those years ago. But, that lapse in judgment also brought me the greatest joy. I prayed that it wasn't too late to save my girls.

As the prayers ended, Gawonii turned his attention to Leotie and Ahyoka.

"Make this tea," Gawonii said as he handed me a packet of dried flowers and bark. "This is dogwood, feverwort, and willow bark. The tea will break the fever."

Grandmother brought over a pot of water that had been warming on the fire. Gawonii administered the tepid tea as Mother and I supported the girls from behind.

"The girls will begin to sweat, and the fever will leave. I need to gather wild cherry bark to aid in healthy bowels. See to the girls until I return."

I cradled Ahyoka in my arms and covered her in blankets while Mother tended to Leotie. I rocked from side to side and sang a song from their infancy.

> *Great Spirit blessed me with two. They will run and play by the water. Two girls are twice the love. They are forever connected.*

"You are strong, my child," I whispered in Ahyoka's ear.

"How is she doing?" Mother asked.

"No different. Let's give the tea some time to set in."

"Leotie is beginning to sweat already. Maybe the fever is leaving," Mother said.

After some time, Leotie's fever left, she sat up by herself and said, "I'm hungry, Mama."

"Let's start with some broth," Grandmother said.

"How is Ahyoka?" Leotie asked.

"Her condition is the same."

"Don't leave me, Sister. I can't live without you," Leotie said. The girls had never been apart. Ahyoka had to survive, or Leotie would die too, not from a fever but of a broken heart. My shoulders slumped forward, and my chin fell to my chest.

Gawonii returned with additional herbs and bark. "I'm thankful to see you up, Leotie. I trust you're feeling better."

"Yes, I'm hungry too."

"That is excellent news. I'm thankful the ministrations are helping. How is Ahyoka doing?"

"Ahyoka's condition hasn't changed," I said.

"I have a stronger tea we can try. One must be careful not to drink too much as boneset can be toxic," Gawonii said. "Start with just a pinch and see how she responds."

My mother made the boneset tea, and I dropped the tea in Ahyoka's mouth a little at a time. Most of it fell out the side of her mouth, yet I continued until Gawonii was satisfied.

"That will do for now. Ahyoka is to drink the boneset tea at sundown and again before sunrise. Meet me at the river at sunrise. For tomorrow, everyone in the village will go to the water in preparation for the Green Corn Festival."

Leotie slept as I watched over Ahyoka. We hoped the morning boneset tea would send the illness out. Mother stoked the fire and prepared the morning teas, cherry wood for Leotie's bowels and boneset for Ahyoka's fever.

"Mama, evil came to my dream again," Leotie said as she woke from her nightmare. "It was awful, Mama. Remember the dream I had when I was sick with a fever?"

"Yes, but you never told me what you dreamt."

"In my first dream, the four of us walked by the riverbank, and a fish jumped on Father and pulled him into the river. He floated away, and the three of us remained. In my dream last night, the three of us walked by the riverbank, and a fish jumped on Ahyoka. She floated away just like Father did. The two of us remained."

"That sounds like a horrible dream," I said. "Let's hope the

Great Spirit has mercy on Ahyoka and changes the outcome of your dream."

"I'm hopeful that going to the river will purify our minds and bodies from all sickness," Leotie said.

"Tea is ready," Grandmother said. "I'll give Ahyoka her tea. I made the tea strong, so the fever will surely leave."

We carried Ahyoka to the river in a blanket; Leotie regained enough strength to walk on her own. We hurried to make it to the river by sunrise. The entire village waited on the riverbank in anticipation of the cleansing ritual. Gawonii approached me with extended arms and said,

"Please, let me take Ahyoka to the water."

I unwrapped the blanket and placed Ahyoka in Gawonii's arms and bowed my head. Gawonii carried her into the river, and the village people followed. He faced the east and immersed himself and Ahyoka. He rose and faced west and went under-water again. The cleansing ritual repeated for a total of seven times, and the people rose from the water purified. I lost sight of Gawonii and Ahyoka as the villagers walked to the riverbank. When the crowd dissipated, I saw Gawonii kneeling over my daughter.

"I'm sorry. I'm sorry, child. I could not save you. May your spirit rise in peace," Gawonii said as he closed Ahyoka's eyes.

"No." I ran to Ahyoka.

"I'm sorry, Amadahy. Her spirit is gone from her body," Gawonii said.

All the women wailed as Leotie and I covered Ahyoka's body with our arms.

"She's cold. She's so cold," Leotie said as she refused to leave Ahyoka. The village women joined us in a lament, repeating her name in anguish.

"Ahyoka, Ahyoka, Ahyoka."

Mother and Grandmother saw us on the ground and came to us as quickly as their time-worn legs would allow. Grand-mother fell to her knees upon seeing Ahyoka's lifeless body.

"It was the tea. You gave her too much boneset tea!" Mother

said.

"No, I would never hurt my great-grandchild."

"You did. You killed Ahyoka, you old buzzard."

"Stop!" I said. "Stop that nonsense."

Grandmother slumped to the ground in despair, and her spirit left her.

The once quiet sunrise ritual turned into hysteria as women wailed, and children were lost in confusion. I closed Grandmother's eyes as the men gathered to discuss what to do. Gawonii approached the elders, and I overheard them talking about when to have the burials as the Green Corn Ceremony was to begin later today.

"Yes, I understand we should honor the first signs of green corn," Gawonii said. "More importantly, we must mourn the loss of an elder and her great-grandchild. We can resume the festival after mourning."

The elders nodded in agreement, and Gawonii called for calm and announced the new plan to the villagers. Several men helped us wrap Ahyoka and grandmother in blankets, and Gawonii led the procession to our home. Mother joined Gawonii, and I stayed with Leotie, who was too distraught to move.

"I'm sorry, Leotie," I said as I brushed the hair out of her face. "I want to take away your pain." The sun moved from the east, and Leotie gathered the strength to walk home.

When we returned, Mother had begun purifying Ahyoka and Grandmother's bodies. Willow root boiled in a medicine pot on the hearth that she later used to cleanse their entire bodies. Mother hurried to be ready for the burial by sundown. I gathered Grandmother's belongings that she needed in the next life, a shell bowl, small animal bones, ceremonial feathers, and clay beads. Mother untied the leather lacing from around grandmother's neck. It carried the wooden charm grandmother claimed had magic powers. She tied the necklace around her own neck rather than putting it with grandmother's belongings.

"Mother, won't Grandmother need her magic charm in the next life?"

"She won't need it, no. I'll tell you of the magic when the time is right."

"Yes, Mother."

Gawonii walked in. "How are the preparations coming?"

"We are finished," Mother said.

"I found a burial site on the east side of the mountain. The slope is covered with pine, a peaceful resting place. They will be laid to rest, together forever," Gawonii said.

"I know it is customary to have an adult accompany you to the burial site, but Leotie is desperate to join us. Would you allow her to come?"

"It is an unusual request. But considering the girls' spirits are closely connected, I can allow it, yes."

"I have Ahyoka's belongings," Leotie said. "Her feathers and blanket."

Mother, Leotie, Gawonii, and I walked to the mountainside. Men of the village carried Grandmother and Ahyoka wrapped in blankets.

"Great Spirit, receive these bodies as they are returned to the ground in the great circle of life," Gawonii said. "Great Spirit, receive their spirits as they are prepared to venture to the next life."

The village men laid the bodies in the mountain tomb with heads facing west. Mother and Leotie put the shell bowls with Grandmother and Leotie's belongings into the grave.

"Mama, it hurts too much. I can't leave her."

"I know it's hard, my precious daughter. This is the greatest pain, and we will get through this somehow, together." I held Leotie, both of us were overcome with grief.

"That's enough," Mother said. "It's time to go home."

I dismissed the anger rising in my chest. My mother could be heartless. But I knew better than to express anger during a time of mourning.

"You cannot return to your home just yet," Gawonii said.

"You need to stay outside tonight. The house is unclean, and I will purify it this evening."

"Yes, Gawonii," Mother said.

She knew not to argue with him. He held our fate in his hands. I trusted Gawonii to do the right thing; Mother trusted no one.

I prepared a broth when we returned home as Gawonii gathered his supplies. I drank broth outside with the remains of my family as Gawonii entered the house with cedar boughs. Home purification was a secret and sacred process, and the old men say it is long and destructive. Smoke billowed from the roof and door as the fire consumed everything we owned.

CHAPTER SEVEN

Janene

Westbrook, North Carolina
2013

The worst thing about a disability is that
people see it before they see you.
– Easter Seals Society

T om and I went to the mall to get a start on Christmas
shopping. Red and green trimmings decked the halls. Silver and gold lights adorned the artificial trees stationed
near the mall entrance. Christmas carols played second fiddle to
the din of cash registers and crowds of excited shoppers.

"Want to stop and get a coffee?" Tom asked.

"A hot, peppermint mocha sounds delicious."

Tom rolled me into Starbucks and found our place in line.
A young mom got in line behind us with a stroller filled with
shopping bags. Strands of hair abandoned her ponytail, and
remnants of lipstick lay stranded on her lips. Her young charge
stood next to her holding her hand.

"Mom, look! A wheelchair," the preschool-aged boy said.

"Shhh, son. That's not nice."

But mom, why is that lady in a wheelchair?"

"Shush."

"But mom."

The young mom backed up and grunted as she wielded the bulky stroller toward the store exit. She pulled the boy's arm as she darted out the door and back into the mayhem of the mall.

"Rude," I said. "Why do parents shush their kids and punish them for being curious?"

Tom shrugged his shoulders and raised an eyebrow.

"I love talking to curious kids. When they ask why I'm in a wheelchair, I tell them it's because my legs don't work. They say, 'Oh, okay,' and don't think twice about it. But when the parents squash questions, I think it sends the wrong message. It's like saying people who are different are inherently defective. Am I crazy for coming to that conclusion?"

"No, that makes sense."

"Grande peppermint mocha for Tom."

Tom rolled me to a table near the door and went back to the counter to get my mocha.

"Here you go, sweetheart. It's nice to spend time with just the two of us, even if we are surrounded by half the residents of North Carolina."

"I've always enjoyed the bustle of the holidays. The shopping, gift wrapping, baking, partying. I'm sorry I can't do much of that anymore," I said with tears welling.

"Don't worry about it. It is what it is, and we can still enjoy what's important – that's being together as a family."

Tom reached out and squeezed my hands. That's his silent way of telling me he loves me. With a full heart, I felt comforted knowing that Tom was there for me no matter what hardships were lurking in the future.

I noticed an elderly couple sitting together without sharing a word. It's as though the two could read each other's thoughts. I was envious that Tom and I may not experience our old age together; I may be long gone before our golden years. The couple gathered their belongings and headed back to the multitudes.

The elderly woman approached me with a smile, tilted her head, and said, "How nice that you can get out of the house, my dear. That's just wonderful."

She patted me on the head and shuffled away. I felt the warmth rise from my chest up through my face. Tears ran down my cheeks.

"Are you kidding me?" I mumbled through clenched teeth. "I can't believe people think I'm an idiot, and it's a miracle when I get out of the house."

"Oh, man. I'm sorry," Tom said. "I think she meant well. She has no idea how condescending that sounded."

"The absolute worst is when people talk about me like I'm not in the room. Seriously? The wheelchair doesn't reduce my IQ to a vegetative state. I'm still me. I'm not this stupid wheelchair, I'm still me."

The dark cloud following me multiplied to a torrential storm pressing down on my chest. The antidepressants were as helpful as an umbrella during a hurricane. This was taking a toll on me. I needed help transferring, and my hands were clumsy and weak. At this rate, I'd say I have a few months left before I'm entirely dependent on someone else to take care of me.

"I'd like to visit Grandma Betty. I think a trip to the coast would do wonders for me, and Grandma always helps me keep things in perspective. Plus, she's 97, and I don't know how much longer she's going to be around."

"She's probably too frail to help you, and I'm falling behind at work."

"Maybe Hannah could come with me for a few days."

"That might work."

Tom and I returned home with our Christmas shopping nearly complete. Daniel was grazing through the refrigerator one leftover at a time.

"Dang, son. Save something for the rest of us," Tom said.

Daniel grabbed an apple from the fruit bowl on his way to the living room without saying a word. My once happy son ignored us and walked away without attempting to snoop through the shopping bags. I felt dismissed.

Hannah walked into the kitchen. "How was the mall?"

"Busy, but we are close to being done with Christmas shopping."

"I'm done," Tom said. "I'm not going back to the mall until Christmas is long gone."

"Hannah, do you have any plans for next weekend? I'd love to go to the coast and visit Grandma Betty for a few days. Would you be willing to go with me?"

"That would be awesome. I love Grandma Betty. She's so much fun."

"Fantastic. I'll give her a call."

During my early childhood, we spent a few weeks every summer on the beach at Grandma Betty's house. Tom and I carried on the tradition with Hannah and Daniel. Grandma's house was much more than a place to visit. It represented the unconditional love and support of family. No matter what, Grandma Betty loved me. She never judged or let on that she was disappointed in me. She trusted that I would figure things out. Sure enough. Well, I hadn't figured this out yet. A trip to Grandma's house was just what the doctor ordered.

The phone rang ten times before Grandma Betty answered. "Hello?"

"Hi, Grandma. It's Janene."

"Hello, sweetheart."

"Oh, Gram, I miss you. Hannah and I want to come and see you next weekend. Are you going to be home?"

"Oh, yes, please. I would love to see you both."

"You're the best, Gram. Love you. See you next week."

We left for the coast early Saturday morning. Tom put our bags into the back seat and asked, "Do you guys have water and snacks for the drive?"

"I packed some almonds and jerky, filled our water bottles too," Hannah said.

"I'm guessing you will get there around 3:00. Text me when you arrive."

"Will do."

"Love you, ladies, to the moon and back," Tom said as he

kissed me through the window and walked over and gave Hannah a hug. "Drive safely. I don't want anything to happen to my favorite women."

"Love you too, Dad," Hannah said as she got into the driver's seat and clicked her seatbelt in place.

Hannah drove down Riparian Drive, and I thought about the stories of our neighbors as we drove past the suburban tract homes. The ample lawns left just enough space for secrets and pain to stay on their own side of the yard. I desperately hoped the storm clouds would stay in Westbrook while we made our escape to the coast. Yet, they joined us. I was determined to enjoy the next few days with Hannah and Grandma Betty in spite of the persistent darkness laying claim to my joy. Time spent with Grandma on the coast will help clear my head.

I looked at Hannah and smiled. "Thanks for coming with me."

"Happy to, Mom. I'm looking forward to seeing Grandma and taking a few days off."

I exhaled and rested my head on the car window. Westbrook was behind us in minutes. The manifold beauty of the Smoky Mountains in the fall allured my senses. Bouquets of red, orange and yellow dotted the slopes. I rolled down my window and inhaled the earthy scent. The smell reminded me of better days as a child playing all day at the river. Did God speak this beauty into existence? If so, how ironic. God created me and this landscape – my failing body and the decaying foliage. Yet, there is beauty in nature's plan and nothing but grief and suffering for me. Where was my beauty? I wasn't a fan of God's plan. No joy for me, only misery. God can kiss my ass.

I rolled up the window, reached over, and placed my hand on Hannah's leg and gave her a squeeze. Hannah glanced down at my hand.

"Wow, Mom. That doesn't even look like your hand. Does it hurt?"

"It hurts when the muscle spasms. But other than that, not really."

"I'm so sorry you're going through this. I can't imagine."

"It is awful. I'm trying to walk through it as best I can. But I'm not handling it very well."

I looked at Hannah and noticed tears falling from under her sunglasses. I felt her pain. I knew all too well what it's like to be a teenager without a mom. I shuddered at the thought of doing the same to Hannah. I exhaled and wished I could quit burdening Hannah with my pain and focus on enjoying the time we had together. I disguised my anguish with a happy face.

"Let's put on some music. What do you feel like listening to?"

"I brought my new Zoey Blue CD." Hannah reached for the console, put the CD into the player, and turned up the volume. We sang the chorus at the top of our lungs.

"Look up! Better days are coming. Don't let the haters bring you down, down, down. Don't let them bring you down."

We laughed and reminisced.

"Remember singing on the way to kindergarten?"

"How much is that doggie in the window?" Hannah said.

"You sang that song every time we walked past the Thomas house. What was the name of that dachshund who barked at us through the picture window?"

"Snoopy."

"You were the cutest kid."

"We had some good times."

The mountains were behind us, and the road led us closer to Grandma's house. I rolled down the window as we entered town. A blast of ocean air greeted my cheeks and transported me to childhood. Cousins played until we passed out on our parents' laps around the beach fire pit. Aunts and uncles stayed up late, laughed, and shared stories of their childhood on the beach. Grandma Betty, the matriarch, made sure the family memories stayed alive and that everyone behaved themselves.

We turned into the driveway, and the white, wooden screen door slapped behind Betty as she wiped her hands on her apron and navigated the wooden steps.

"Hello, hello, hello!" Betty said.

Hannah put the car in park and jumped out to hug Betty.

"Hi, Grandma!"

Hannah paused as she felt Betty's shoulder blades protruding from her once-robust frame. Betty was a 5'2" force to be reckoned with. Don't be fooled by her short stature. Even with her recent frailty, there was no doubt, Betty was large and in charge.

"Oh, Hannah. You've grown into a beautiful young woman, just like your momma and grandma."

"Aw, thanks, Gram. Let me get Mom out of the car."

Hannah started the familiar routine of getting the wheelchair out of the trunk and transferring me from the car to the wheelchair.

"My stars, Janene. What is all of this?"

"I don't know, Gram. My legs aren't working."

"Oh, dear, I'm so sorry. I didn't know it was this bad."

"I'm a hot mess! I could sure use some Grandma time."

"I'm here for you, sweetheart."

Hannah unloaded the car and rolled me into the back yard. Betty joined us on the lawn with some sweet iced tea.

"How'd you do it, Grandma?" I asked.

"Do what, dear?"

"How did you manage to keep going after the accident? You lost your husband, daughter, and son-in-law that day because someone decided to drive drunk."

"Oh, sweetie, I grieved somethin' fierce. But I had you. You were so precious. What were you? Thirteen years old?"

"Yes, thirteen. I barely remember my parents, but I remember that day. I know you had to take care of me, but how did you handle the grief?"

"I don't like to dwell on the past, Janene."

"I know. But, I'm struggling and could use your advice."

Betty held out her hands and examined the toll years had taken on her joints and skin.

"I wanted to cry myself to sleep and never get out of bed again. The loss was unbearable. But what choice did I have? If I had given up, I would have dishonored the memories of those who died. They would have wanted me to live. I wanted to get up in the morning to take care of you. You gave me a reason to live."

"That sounds like a miraculous recovery," I said.

"Not at all, dear. It was weeks, months, and years of taking it one day at a time."

"I like that, Grandma. One day at a time." Hannah shifted in her seat and drew a long drink of tea.

Betty fixed her gaze on the ocean, and the three of us sat in silence. It wasn't an awkward nor pregnant pause, rather a contented moment. The sound of the incoming tide reminded me of water's resilience. An evaporated drop of water gathers strength by joining forces in a cloud, only to reappear in a new form, in a new place. One drop, one day at a time.

Grandma Betty turned to me, "What's going on, Janene?"

"I'm afraid, Gram. I don't have any control over what's happening. I feel like I'm losing my mind."

"I hear you, and I can hear the fear in your voice." Betty took a sip of tea. "Can anyone control what happens?"

Betty returned her glass to the table. Hannah and I leaned in to hear Betty answer her own question.

"We are all one accident, illness, or job loss away from personal disaster. No, you can't control what happens to you. You will drive yourself crazy if you think you can."

"What can you control?" Hannah asked.

"The only thing you can control is how you respond," Betty said.

After several minutes, Betty stood up and steadied herself.

"I'll be right back. I have something I want to show you. I believe the time has come."

Hannah and I looked at each other with curiosity.

"I hope what she wants to give me is some sage advice on how to cope with grief," I said. "What do you think?"

"I have no idea. But, it's safe to say Grandma will know what to do."

We smiled and leaned back into our chairs. The breeze and

the soothing sound of ocean waves proved to be a salve for my soul.

Betty returned, clutching a small box in her hand. "Here we go," she said as she sat down. "I'm going to share a secret that has helped women for centuries."

Hannah and I sat at the edge of our seats to see what Grandma held so dear.

"This will help you feel better," Betty said as she placed a small wooden box in front of me. "This is for you."

"How thoughtful, thank you."

"Aren't you going to open it?" Betty said.

I looked to Hannah to open it.

Hannah's smile spread ear-to-ear as she opened the wooden box. She pulled the necklace chain and grasped the silver charm in the palm of her hand.

"Oh, Grandma. It's beautiful."

"That smile confirms it," Betty said. "Do you see the repeating silhouette of a woman? That represents the passage of this special charm down the maternal line."

"Bring it closer, Hannah, so I can see," I said.

"See it right here?" Hannah said as she pointed to the charm.

"Yes, I've never seen anything like it," I said.

Betty drew close and whispered to me, "This is a talisman with special powers. Don't tell a soul about it."

I raised my eyebrows, asking her to tell me more.

"Shush. Don't say a word, either of you." Betty wagged her finger. "You will know how to access its secret power when the time is right."

Hannah secured the chain around my neck and centered the charm upon my chest. "There you go."

CHAPTER EIGHT

Cora

Westbrook, North Carolina
1873

We accept the love we think we deserve.
– Stephen Chbosky

T he war had ended, but battles still raged. We, as a people, had our freedom from being owned, yet we were far from equal in the eyes of men and the law. No one on the Yarbrough Plantation cared enough to search for my dead body all those years ago. So I escaped into obscurity and became just another Negro orphan taken in by Miss Hattie. I reaped the benefits of growing through my teen years with a free woman. You would be hard-pressed to find anyone more grateful than me in all of Westbrook. She taught me how to read and write and how to navigate the white man's world.

"Always speak respectfully and keep your head low," Hattie said. "Don't draw attention to yourself in a way that gets a man's eye. But don't let anyone walk on you. Be proud of who you are."

Hattie used humor and flattery to get what she needed, but she stood her ground. One time she made breakfast of biscuits and gravy for 35 soldiers who were holed up in Westbrook. I'll never forget that morning. I was hanging clothes on the line and listening to the finches squabble. I heard the sound of boots marching on the dirt and gravel road. I held on to a damp apron I was about to pin on the line as I strained to make sense of what I heard.

I walked to the side of the house, hoping to see what was happening without being seen. Lines of men in gray wool jackets marched down Main Street. Run, child. Run! I heard Mama Ada say. Men in gray wool jackets killed innocents and made me a whore. I held the apron in front of me to shield myself. They couldn't hurt me now.

"Company, halt!" The man on the horse said, and the boots on the road stopped marching in the middle of town. "I will dismiss you to find water and shade, and I will find food for your bellies. Company, dismissed."

Rows of haggard men walked to the side of the road, some lay in the dirt without concerning themselves with shade. I went inside the house to find Hattie.

"Mama, hungry soldiers marched into town. The man on the horse said he was looking for food."

"Cora, fetch some fresh milk and fill your apron with eggs. I'll go have a talk with the man on the horse."

Hattie walked out the front door, and I went to milk the cow. When I returned to the kitchen with milk and eggs, Hattie had sifted every bit of flour from the larder.

"Start on the gravy, Cora. We've got to feed 35 soldiers. They ran out of food days ago, and the man on the horse agreed to pay three cents for each soldier fed."

We made biscuits and gravy, and the men in gray wool jackets ate their rations. When breakfast ended, the soldiers gathered their belongings and lined up to march out of town. That's when Hattie walked straight to the man on the horse.

"You look satisfied, sir. Did you enjoy your breakfast? I believe the good Lord said in Exodus 20 and 15, thou shalt not steal. I'd be much obliged good sir, for the payment of $1.05."

The man could not deny her truth and paid the total sum before departing. The soldiers cheered to celebrate Hattie's breakfast.

The Bible was my favorite book to read. Miss Hattie said that the Bible had the answer to any question.

"Who are we in Christ Jesus?" Hattie asked.

"There is neither Jew nor Greek, there is neither bond nor free, there is neither male nor female: for ye are all one in Christ Jesus," I said. "Galatians 3 and 28."

"That's right. And what can you do?"

"I can do all things through Christ which strengtheneth me. Philippians 4 and 13."

"That's right. And, who is the Lord?"

"The Lord is my shepherd; I shall not want. Psalm 23 and 1."

"That's right. And why don't you want?"

"God shall supply all my needs according to his riches in glory by Christ Jesus. Philippians 4 and 19."

"That's right. And, don't forget sweet Cora, that I love you and Jesus loves you too."

Although I knew the word of the Lord by heart, I must have not believed it in my heart. I didn't experience the peace of God, which passeth all understanding. Don't get me wrong, I felt safe in Mama Hattie's home. Eli and Lewis protected me, yet I felt uncertain. Times were changing, and I didn't know what to do or expect. Mama Hattie told me it was time to look for a husband and that I didn't have to look too far. I did notice Eli making himself known.

Mama Hattie never remarried after her beloved Elijah, Sr. died in the battle to take Cumberland Gap. Hattie survived, some would say she thrived, by teaching the town's Negro children. Oftentimes, grown children return the generosity Hattie had shown them. "The Lord will provide," Hattie declared. The household stayed busy since Hattie had taken in children orphaned by the war. More mouths to feed and more washing to do. So many children needed homes, far more than we could help.

Eli and Lewis had permanent jobs at the mill and carried their own weight. They were grown men and eager to strike out on their own. I was grown too. What was next for me? My household chores and helping Hattie with school kept me occupied for now. But in the back of my mind, I heard my Mama Ada telling me I was born for more. I reached for the comfort of my necklace. Ada said she would tell me about its magical power when the time was right, but we ran out of time years ago.

I sat on the back steps to rest and consider the spring planting; corn, squash, and green beans to the left. I thought more tomatoes and fewer cukes on the right. Potatoes and greens thrived where they've been for years. This bountiful garden fed Miss Hattie's family, countless children, and soldiers from the north and south. Hattie and I preserved a few vegetables like Mama Ada had taught me years ago. We often traded our extra vegetables with other families to enjoy a variety of food.

Eli came outside and motioned his desire to join me. I scooted over to make room on the step.

"Beautiful evening," Eli said.

"Yes. I'm enjoying the sunset." I caught a comforting whiff of sawdust and sweat. Eli and I spent countless hours talking on the back steps, but tonight something felt peculiar. The air fell still, and Eli's words came out shaking. I hoped he wasn't ill.

"Cora, You know I enjoy your company. Would you like to join me for a picnic on Sunday by the river?"

"Just the two of us? That doesn't seem proper."

"I can ask Lewis to join us. He's been itching to spend time with Meriday."

"I think Meriday is a lady and will have no business scratching Lewis's itch," I said as I stood up and playfully pushed Eli's shoulder. "I'll have to ask Mama's permission."

"I know Mama would be pleased," Eli said as I ran inside.

I laid down on my pallet and stared at the roof. A smile grew as I hugged my quilt. I wasn't accustomed to this feeling. I rolled onto my stomach and buried my face hoping to hide these odd feelings. I didn't want the attention Eli sent my way. It distracted me from my work and left me feeling uneasy. Yet, deep down, I yearned to be loved in that unspoken way. No. I knew better. I fell asleep and met Eli in my dreams.

I woke early the next day and tended to the animals. Thank you, hens, for your eggs. Thank you, nannies, for your milk. Thank you, God, for the sunrise. I felt right at home with the animals or alone in the garden. It was where I felt near to God and distant from grief.

Hattie met me in the kitchen, and we prepared breakfast together.

"You look chipper this morning, Cora."

"It's a beautiful day."

The smell of breakfast brought the boys to the kitchen.

"It will be a while before breakfast is ready," Hattie said.

"Can I help in the kitchen?" Eli said.

"I won't say no to that. Get a basket of potatoes from the cellar and scrub them clean."

"Sure thing, Mama. We've got some time before we leave for the mill."

"Lewis," Hattie said. "Get the young ones up and dressed, please."

"Yes, Mama."

Four children made their home with us until Hattie could find them a family. Orphans found a way to Miss Hattie's house, and Hattie managed to find them families. So many children needed a home. I wished we could take in more, but we didn't have room nor food.

"I've been wondering, Mama, why did you keep me? I'm thankful you did, but wondering why."

"That's an easy question, sweet Cora. I'd been praying to the Lord to send me a daughter, and there you were, sitting in my kitchen. You are an answer to prayer."

"I'm lucky to be your daughter."

"You were a brave young girl, running away from those bad men. Brave, indeed."

"I've got another question. Eli wants to take me on a picnic Sunday. Lewis and Meriday want to come too. Can I have your permission to go?"

"I think that is a lovely idea. We can fry up some chicken."

"It feels strange, Mama. Eli has been kind to me since the morning he found me under that tree. But this is different. I don't know what to make of it."

"That's understandable. You all are grown now, and Eli is sweet on you."

"I'm not sure I've time for that."

"Give him a chance, Cora. He's a good man."

"Yes, Mama."

Sunday morning came, and Mama helped me prepare the picnic. Food, plates, and a blanket all packed in a basket.

"Your hands are trembling like a bride," Hattie said. "Come, give me a hug."

I melted into Hattie's embrace as Eli and Lewis bound into the kitchen.

"Are you ready?" Lewis asked.

"Here's your picnic," Hattie said. "Have a good time and be home before the sun goes down, or I'll send out a search party."

"Yes, Mama," Lewis said.

Eli took the picnic basket, and we headed down the road to Meriday's house. Lewis walked ahead of us eager to meet Meriday. Eli's arm brushed against mine, giving me a case of the shivers. He smiled and glanced at me from the corner of his eye. I took a step to the left, leaving room between us. Meriday sat waiting on the front porch when we arrived at her house. She wore a blue shawl tied around her shoulders. I felt foolish in my patched apron. She joined us on the road, and we continued our walk to the river.

"Here's the perfect spot," Eli said.

He spread out the blanket, and the four of us enjoyed Hattie's fried chicken and boiled ears of corn. Baked cinnamon apples topped the satisfying meal. Meriday giggled as Lewis whispered in her ear. They stood up and walked hand-in-hand down the riverbank and out of sight. I busied myself cleaning up the picnic, knowing I could stay a safe distance from Eli if my hands weren't idle. Mama Ada used to say, "Idle hands make the devil's job easy." I wanted no part of that. I knew what I was, and I would only bring shame to Eli.

"Here, let me help you with that."

Eli placed his hands on mine, leaned in, and kissed me on the cheek. I startled when I felt a tingle between my legs. I pulled back and swept the feeling under the rug as quickly as it came.

"Please, no."

"I'm sorry," Eli said. "I didn't mean to upset you. I find you irresistible and hope you feel the same about me."

"Oh, Eli. No one has been more kind to me than you. But I'm not ready for this. Take me home, please."

I finished packing the picnic basket, flushed with embarrassment, and holding back tears. Eli walked down the riverbank calling for Lewis and Meriday. They appeared from the bushes a little ruffled but clothed. The young lovers whispered and giggled all the way home. Eli and I walked along in silence. I couldn't hide my apprehension, and Eli's posture didn't hide his disappointment.

I didn't see much of Eli in the following weeks as he spent his evenings fishing at the river. He appeared lonely as his best friend and younger brother spent every free moment with Meriday. It came as no surprise when Lewis announced his plans to marry.

"Lewis, that is wonderful news," Hattie said. "When are you going to jump the broom?"

"Next month. First, I need to find a place we can call home. Mr. Morgan has a cabin on the river near the mill. It needs some work. Thank goodness my brother is handy with a hammer."

"You are always welcome here," Hattie said.

"Congratulations, brother," Eli said. "Meriday is a fine

woman."

"Thanks. I feel like the luckiest man alive."

Lewis and Meriday married on a Saturday. Reverend Walker officiated the ceremony on the riverbank, under the shade of an old dogwood tree. Meriday wore a simple white dress with faux pearl buttons. Eli stood next to Lewis, and I stood with Meriday. Hattie beamed as she welcomed her new daughter to the family. Meriday's uncle played the fiddle as we ate our fill and danced in celebration.

I sat on a stone ledge to take a break from the festivities. Eli joined me a few minutes later.

"What a day," Eli said.

"Yes. I'm happy for the new couple."

"Cora, I've loved you since the day I met you. I've been in love with you since you've become a woman. I can't imagine spending my life with anyone but you."

"Eli," I said.

"Hear me out, Cora. If you marry me, I promise to spend every day of my life committed to you and our children. Will you, will you marry me, Cora?"

I buried my face in my hands, hoping to hide my tears.

"I can't, Eli. I'm so sorry. I can't marry you."

"Why, Cora? Why can't you marry me? What have I done wrong that you refuse me?"

"It's not you, Eli. It's me. I can't."

I didn't dare to tell Eli that he deserved someone better. I was made a whore, broken and dirty. I didn't deserve to be known or loved by a man like Eli.

"I don't understand why you can't love me," Eli said as he walked away, head down, arms hanging.

Hattie didn't understand either. "You'll never find a better man, Cora."

"I know, Mama," I said. "I think I'm destined to never marry."

"Why, pray tell, would you say such a thing?"

"I don't know, Mama."

The terror of that evil day my family died held me hostage.

The chains weren't visible, but the bondage was unmistakable.

Supper time conversations didn't stray beyond the weather and daily gossip from the market. So, Eli's announcement came as a surprise.

"I'm leaving Westbrook and moving east. Talk at the mill is that there's new folks setttling in Ashville and they need more builders."

"That could be a good opportunity for you," Hattie said. "But, I'm not going to lie and say I'm happy that you're leaving Westbrook."

"They said all men are welcome, white and Negro. I'll work hard and learn new skills. Besides, nothing is keeping me here," Eli said as he glanced my way.

CHAPTER NINE

Amadahy

Aguaquiri
Flower Moon, 1664

Love is like the wind, you can't see it, but you can feel it.
– Nicholas Sparks

I didn't have the means to pay Gawonii for all his services, no woven blankets or leather garments as I lost everything in the purification fire. Gawonii forgave my debt, but I felt obligated to repay him. I used my connection to the earth to repay his kindness. The medicine man needed an abundance of flowers and plants to meet the physical and spiritual needs of the villagers. Leotie and I found solace together in the meadow.

"Remember to pick every fourth lavender plant."

"Yes, Mama. I know."

"The sun feels comforting today. How are you, Leotie?"

"I feel broken, like half of my spirit is missing. I miss her so much."

"I know you do. I miss Ahyoka too."

"But we have to keep living, keep trying," Leotie said.

"Hush," I said.

I heard someone or something moving nearby. I squatted and signaled Leotie to do likewise. We sat motionless and in silence. Leotie's eyes were wide with fear. I looked into her eyes and covered my mouth, telling her to be quiet. My heart raced, and my senses quickened. Village men reported seeing strangers with pale skin and short hair while out hunting. No one has had direct contact with strangers, and I was not eager to be the first. The thrashing grew louder, and a surge of power rushed through my body. No one or nothing was going to hurt or separate me from my only child.

Was it a man with pale skin or a hostile warrior from a southern tribe? I looked over the lavender towards the river and saw the one who frightened me. It was a tall, slender woman who seemed to be Cherokee but not of my Wolf Clan. She was harvesting river cane. Her back muscles shone with sweat as she reached for the top of the plants. I was mesmerized by the rhythmic beauty of her harvest. My spirit did not feel a threat, so I rose from my makeshift hiding place and said, "Osiyo."

She turned toward us and said, "Hello. I hope I'm not disturbing you."

"No," I said as I walked closer with Leotie a few steps behind me. The stranger pulled a woven mat full of harvested river cane. "What is your clan? We wear similar skins, but I've never seen you before."

"My people are from the Bear Clan to the southwest."

I circled the woman as I spoke. "I am called Amadahy of the Wolf Clan. What brings you from the safety of your people to this part of the river?"

"I am Quatsey, the weaver. I've followed the river north to harvest river cane. Nowhere is it more plentiful than here. I must return home now."

Quatsey loaded the last of the river cane on her mat, turned around, and walked away.

Leotie and I loaded our feeble baskets and walked toward Gawonii's home.

"Quatsey could teach us to make baskets that last more than a season," Leotie said.

"You're right, Leotie. We could learn from her."

We returned to the village and presented the lavender to Gawonii.

"Thank you, Amadahy. You have a gift for harvesting the finest medicine."

His words penetrated my darkness like a ray of sunshine breaks through the clouds. Quatsey remained on my mind as Leotie and I walked home. Mother was boiling meat on the fire when we returned. It was too early for maize or squash, but Leotie and I found ripe blackberries in the meadow today.

"Hello, Mother."

"I was alone until the snakes came. Black snakes crawled in through the firestones on the floor. They slithered into every basket and pot, every bowl and pelt. They hissed at me with their forked tongues, pure evil."

"Are the snakes still here?" Leotie asked.

"I threatened to boil them, and that was enough to scare them away."

I folded the pelts and stacked the bowls and baskets strewn throughout the house, a familiar task after Mother's imagined invasions. Last time, she saved us from spiders.

"We need new baskets and mats. You are a disappointment, Amadahy. A bear cub could weave a better basket than you."

"We met a gifted weaver today who was harvesting river cane," I said.

"She's a basket weaver from the Bear Clan to the southwest," Leotie said. "I told Mama maybe we could learn from her."

"We do need help with weaving," Mother said.

"Mama, why don't we take a trip down the river and see if we can find Quatsey?" Leotie said.

"Well, that's an interesting idea. What do you think, Mother?"

"There are bad spirits and bad people outside of the village."

"There are bad spirits in the village and in this house too," Leotie said.

"That may be true, Leotie, but you must speak respectfully in this house and to your elders."

"Yes, Mama. But I think we should go on this journey to find Quatsey. We could learn so much from her."

"I agree. Improving our weaving skills would be a blessing to the entire village."

"I think the two of you are young and foolish."

"I've always been your fool, Mother." Foolish or not, the thought of seeing Quatsey stirred excitement within me.

"Don't be angry, Mother."

"I'm not angry. I just don't understand your ways."

Mother shook her head and tended to her cooking as Leotie and I gathered provisions for the upcoming journey. Berries and dried meat, blankets for sleeping, beads for trading. What else? A canoe, that will be the most efficient way to travel.

"Leotie, let's go borrow a canoe."

"Who is unwise and will give you a canoe?" Mother asked. "You should find a man to go with you."

"I appreciate your concern. But I think Leotie and I can take care of ourselves. I'll ask Gawonii about borrowing his canoe."

I found Gawonii at home with his mortar and pestle grinding dried flowers.

"Good evening, I hope you are well."

"I'm certainly occupied with all the medicine you have provided."

"I come asking a favor. I need to borrow your canoe."

"Of course, Amadahy. May I ask where you are going?"

"Leotie and I are going south to find Quatsey, the weaver. We want to learn new weaving skills."

"That will be quite an adventure. Are you sure you want to travel outside of the village, just you and a child?"

"I'm aware of the danger, but feel this journey is worth the risk."

"My canoe and oars are outside. I will say a blessing over your travels."

"Thank you. I'll bring you beautiful baskets when we return."

I thought about the dangers lurking outside – men, animals, rapids. Was seeing Quatsey again worth the risk? Was it unwise to bring Leotie on the journey? The only thing I knew for sure was that I was unable to deny my desire to see Quatsey again.

"Do you want to go with me, Leotie?"

"I love adventures. Ahyoka and I used to go on adventures together. Plus, Grandma is not happy, and I'd rather not be alone with her."

"I understand. Ahyoka's spirit will journey with us."

"Yes, Mama."

Leotie and I walked home with grief as our companion. I made final preparations for our trip and laid down with precious Leotie until we fell asleep.

The eastern sun shone through the cracks in the wall, and I nudged Leotie awake.

"Leotie, let's go."

"Yes, Mama."

I took in the morning air, each breath cleansing my spirit.

"Thank you, Great Spirit. I'm grateful for this day. Bless our travels down the river."

Leotie and I loaded provisions into the canoe and carried it to the river. The birds accompanied us with their morning songs as we walked through the valley, and the smell of wet earth greeted my nose as we neared the river. I launched the canoe with Leotie inside. I inhaled through my teeth when my feet hit the chilled water. I pushed into the current and hopped in. I slipped the end of the oar into the water and began our journey.

"Mama, it's so peaceful. I feel Ahyoka's spirit with us."

"I welcome her adventurous spirit on our journey. "

I felt connected to the Great Spirit as we floated down the river. I felt free from judgment and grief. This might have been a sign that balance returned to my life. I watched Leotie take in her surroundings. Her developing body was leaving childhood behind. I wanted time to stop, so Leotie would never face the pain and suffering of womanhood; she suffered enough losing her twin. In that present moment, I returned my attention to Leotie and the joy emanating from her. This was the first time

I'd seen Leotie smile since Ahyoka died. The mourning period tested our resolve to keep living, keep searching for purpose. Meeting Quatsey by the river signaled a new beginning for my life, new meaning and purpose. Did I dishonor the memory of my daughter by wanting to move on with life? Ahyoka would not want us to live in sadness.

We came to a clearing in the riverbank when the sun was at its highest.

"Let's stop here to eat and stretch our legs."

I steered the canoe toward the landing. Leotie grabbed the food basket and stepped out of the canoe.

"I'm hungry," Leotie said. "This looks like the perfect place to stop."

"Me too," I said as I pulled the canoe onto the bank. We enjoyed some dried meats and berries in the sunshine. Leotie got up to relieve herself.

"I'll be right back, Mama."

I locked my fingers behind my head, leaned back, and closed my eyes. The sun warmed my face as I rested. Moments later, I heard the sounds of an animal snorting and scratching. I lay motionless, and imperceptibly opened my eyes. Hoping to see a beaver or fox, I was terrified to see a brown bear sitting in our canoe. I prayed Leotie would walk with caution and respect in the unfamiliar land as to not startle the bear. So far, I didn't see or hear any signs of her return. The bear left the canoe and moved toward me. I listened to my heart beating and focused on breathing without moving.

The bear found our meat and berries we hoped would last us for the journey. Gone. Still curious, the bear lumbered toward me as I lay in repose. It paused and sniffed my toes and up my legs. I pictured Leotie dragging my body parts into the canoe and paddling home upstream. It stopped and snorted on my belly. I felt the warm saliva splatter on my skin. The bear stood on its hind legs and growled. Just as the bear's claw swept down to disembowel me, it stopped and turned toward the river as a stone broke the water's surface. A second stone dropped into the river. Maybe the possibility of fresh fish piqued its interest more than a sinewy human. Whatever the reason, the bear left me and returned to the river. I waited. Was my lack of movement born of wisdom or being frozen by fear? I think the latter.

I sat up as Leotie ran toward me from behind a growth of reeds.

"Mama, you're alive! I thought you were dead."

Leotie threw her arms around me and sobbed.

"I'm okay, Leotie. I'm okay."

We held each other until the fear subsided, and our breathing slowed.

"I worried that you would come back, and the bear would go after you."

"You taught me that everything is sacred, even stones. So, I thanked the stones for helping me distract the bear and threw them in the river," Leotie said as her breathing slowed.

"I'm proud of you, Leotie. You saved my life."

"I was afraid, Mama. The thought of losing you was more than I could bear."

"It's going to be okay. Let's clean this mess and continue our journey."

Leotie picked up the food basket and giggled.

"Look what the bear did to our basket."

"Quatsey will really want to help us now," I said.

We laughed and hugged. Holding Leotie was the best medicine for the emotional war that raged within me. We gathered our provisions and wits and continued our travels. I exhaled as the oar broke the water's tension, and I was grateful to be moving again.

"I think we are close, Leotie. Do you see any signs of people?"

"There's an opening on the bank that looks like people have been there. See how the grass is trampled?"

"You have a sharp eye, Leotie."

I held the oar tight on my left and guided the canoe to the clearing. We secured the canoe and set out to find Quatsey. Leotie led the way as we walked without disturbing the ground or a bird. The trail became obvious the longer we walked. Leo-tie stopped and covered her mouth with her right hand and pointed to her left ear. I listened and heard nothing. Leotie's young ears heard things I didn't. We continued along the trail in silence. Leotie stopped and looked at a growth of bushes to the north as five young men stepped out with arrows drawn. The eldest pointed his bow down and asked,

"What is your purpose here?"

"My name is Amadahy, from the Wolf Clan to the north. I come looking for Quatsey, the basket weaver."

The man signaled for others to lower their weapons and said, "Welcome, Amadahy, I will take you to Quatsey."

"Thank you." Leotie and I followed the men to the village. My knees weakened at the thought of seeing Quatsey again.

CHAPTER TEN

Janene

Westbrook, North Carolina
2014

Hope is being able to see that there is light despite
all of the darkness.
— Desmond Tutu

T om and I drove to Ashville for my neurology appointment. I was anxious for an answer, yet, dreaded what it
could be. The sun shone, and I relished the time Tom
and I spent alone. We both had busy careers and different social
outlets; Hannah and Daniel brought us together. We'd made our
share of mistakes, but raising kids together was our crowning
achievement. We looked forward to retirement, traveling together. Then, best of all, we looked forward to grandkids. I've
heard they are the reward for surviving parenthood.

Traffic increased as we got closer to the city; sedans, pickups,
and commercial trucks filled the interstate lanes. Square build-
ings of brick and glass sprouted through lush, green trees. I welcomed the scenic change from my small, riverside town. It provided a brief respite, uncurling my white-knuckled fists. Tom
followed the voice of his GPS navigation. As we approached the
hospital, I felt overwhelmed with relief and trepidation at the

thought of receiving a diagnosis.

We pulled into the parking garage and searched for an accessible spot. I smelled car exhaust and saw its black stains painted on the concrete walls. I wondered how many other patients had parked their cars in this garage to hear life-altering news. I feared I would join them. Tom rolled me toward the hospital, and automatic doors opened, greeting us like expected guests. Elderly people dressed in layers occupied the lobby chairs. Some had walkers sitting alongside them like obedient pets. Textured plastic runners protected the blue commercial carpet, and framed posters of smiling patients adorned the walls.

We rolled to the elevators and found Dr. Winters' name listed under neurology, suite 415, on the hospital directory. The ding of an arriving elevator caught my attention. Tom backed my chair into the elevator, and a host of irrational thoughts crossed the threshold with me. We are going to get stuck in here. I'm never going to walk again. This lady is standing too close to my face. That guy is going to sneeze contagions all over me.

"Fourth floor," said a woman's voice coming from an elevator speaker. The unique sound of her voice interrupted my thoughts.

Tom checked in at the reception desk, and we waited to be escorted to an exam room. A handsome, young man with dark eyes and matching wavy hair, entered the lobby. "Mrs. Branch, Janene Branch?"

"Yes, that's me."

"This way, please."

We entered a small room, and the man in scrubs sat in front of a keyboard and said, "Hi. My name is Mike. I'll be taking your medical history and getting you ready for some tests with Dr. Winters. Okay?"

I looked at him in affirmation. When Mike finished his tasks, he said, "Dr. Winters will see you shortly."

Dr. Winters, a tall, slender man, entered the room. "Hello, Janene. I'm Bob Winters. I've looked over your history and current concerns. I'd like to run some tests and see if we can determine what's going on. Let's have a look."

I followed his directions as best I could and muffled my cries of pain. He ran electrical pulses through my nerves. Then he repeatedly stuck my muscles with needles that were attached to wires, sending data to a console on a metal cart.

"I'm sorry this is painful, Janene. We're almost finished. You're doing great."

I presented calmly, but my mind cycled through worst-case scenarios.

"All right. We're done with the exam. How are you doing?"

"I'm glad that's over."

"I'm going to review the results with my team. Go ahead and relax. I'll be back shortly."

Tom pulled out his phone, and I pushed back my cuticles while we waited.

Dr. Winters tapped on the exam room door and made his second entrance. His white coat provided little contrast to his disheveled white hair and pale skin. Worn, leather shoes revealed countless walks into exam rooms to deliver devastating news. He reviewed my nerve conduction and EMG tests, loosely held in a red folder. He rubbed his chin and exhaled, turning attention to me. The scent of hand sanitizer wafted to my nose. He rolled his stool toward me, intruding into my personal space bubble.

"It's not looking good, Janene."

I looked at the floor, tears flooded my eyes. Dr. Winters mustered a sympathetic face and inched his stool closer.

"You've got muscle weakness and atrophy in both your arms and legs. Other conditions have been ruled out and my tests today confirm that you have ALS. I'm sorry, Janene."

All I heard was white noise, my vision blurred, a scream caught in my throat. My worst nightmare became a reality. A terminal diagnosis, a death sentence in two to five years. Nothing could stop my motor neurons from dying, leaving me unable to move, swallow, speak, or breathe. Dear God, why me? What had I done to deserve this?

"I suggest you travel, or do whatever is on your bucket list and get your affairs in order," Dr. Winters said.

I'd spent my life teaching and taking care of kids. Wasn't that good enough? Why punish me like this? I took care of other people, I couldn't fathom others taking care of me. Dying on the inside, thoughts of a slow, suffocating death consumed me.

The Jaws of Life couldn't extract Tom's thoughts. He sat motionless with his head down and elbows resting on his knees. His hands clasped with his fingers intertwined. His distant hazel eyes looked up and he asked,

"What does this all mean?"

Dr. Winters explained, "ALS, Amyotrophic Lateral Sclerosis, is a neurodegenerative disease that causes the motor neurons, the nerves that control muscles, to atrophy and die. This is not an easy road, but we are here to help Janene stay comfortable."

"Is there anything you can do?" Tom asked.

"I'll write a few prescriptions to help with muscle cramps and pain. We will be enrolling patients in a clinical trial soon. I would encourage you to consider participating, Janene."

"I will."

Dr. Winters placed his hand on my shoulder. "Give the office a call and schedule a clinic visit in about three months."

Tom rolled me into the parking lot and transferred my failing body from the wheelchair into the Camry. I buckled my seatbelt and sighed. The sigh turned into a moan, then sobs. We pulled out of the parking lot and began the four-hour drive west from Durham to Westbrook. This was not how my life was supposed to unfold.

Six weeks later, Tom and I drove to Asheville with renewed hope. Dallas, the research coordinator, called last week to tell me they were enrolling patients in a new stem cell trial and wanted me to come to the clinic right away.

"What do I have to lose?"

Tom said, "I've got questions for Dallas about side effects."

"Maybe I'll grow a third boob or something."

"Now, that's a side effect I can live with."

"I'm really hopeful, Tom. What if this treatment works?"

"Let's see what they have to say."

Rolling into the ALS clinic brought a flood of memories: EMG needles, hand sanitizer, and a terminal diagnosis. We didn't wait long for Dallas to escort us to her office. I steered my new power chair down the hallway with the confidence of a 15-year-old learning to drive. I felt comfortable with Dallas yet apprehensive about the trial.

"Let's get right to it," Dallas said. "This is groundbreaking stuff. We really don't know how or if stem cells will work in ALS. So we have to do clinical trials to find out if it is safe and if it works."

"I've got a lot of questions," Tom said.

"Absolutely, ask away," Dallas said.

I gazed out the window at the busy street below, tuning out the conversation. Look at the people walking and stepping up a curb without giving it a thought. Oh, she just hopped out of a car in high heels. Nice. I wonder if any of the people know how lucky they are. I didn't realize how fortunate I was to be able-bodied until I wasn't.

"Janene, what do you think?" Tom asked. "Janene?"

"Will I be able to walk again?"

"I certainly can't promise that, or any benefit for you at all. You do meet the inclusion criteria, though. It's now up to you to decide if you want to participate." Dallas said.

"Let me think about it."

"Absolutely. We are approved to enroll five patients. Please let me know if you want to participate as soon as possible."

"Thanks, Dallas. I'll give you a call."

"I appreciate you coming in."

Dallas walked us to the reception desk, and Tom and I headed to the parking garage.

"That will be a lot of time in the hospital and away from the kids. Hannah is leaving for college in the fall," I said. "It's too much time for you to take off work."

"We can work that out. I'm more concerned about the 50% placebo. It seems outrageous."

"More like barbaric. It is a lot to go through, the surgeries and hospital stays for only a 50% chance of getting real stem cells. On the other hand, I have a zero percent chance of getting a stem cell treatment if I avoid the risks. I don't feel I have a choice if I want to live."

Hannah and Daniel were home when we returned. Their red, puffy eyes revealed the sadness of their conversation. Maybe it was fear or uncertainty, most likely both.

"How did it go?" Hannah asked as she inhaled and wiped her eyes.

"It is a little overwhelming, but maybe, just maybe, the stem cells could help me."

"So, are you going to get the stem cells?" Daniel asked.

"We've got some logistics to work out first, but we are pretty sure we want to do it," Tom said.

"What kind of logistics?" Daniel asked.

"Mom will need help in the hospital for a week at a time and then someone at home with her."

"We were just talking about that," Hannah said.

"I thought Grandma Betty could move in with us for a while," I said.

"No way," Hannah said. "She won't leave her house. Anyway, she couldn't handle the physical part of caring for you. Not to mention the driving."

"That's true," I said. "We will figure something out."

"About that. I think I should delay college a semester or two and stay home to help you."

"No way, no way," I said. "Your future, your plans. Nothing is more important than that."

"No, Mom. Nothing is more important to me than being with you."

Hannah and I couldn't hold back our tears. I looked up at

Tom over Hannah's shoulder. Tears rolled down his cheeks. Tom grabbed his forehead and sat next to Daniel on the couch. He put his arm around his son. Daniel stood up and waved his arms like a baseball umpire calling a runner safe at home plate.

"This is too much. It's all about you and your problems, Mom. Other people have problems too, you know," Daniel said as he stormed out of the living room and toward the front door.

"Wait! Where are you going?" I asked.

"I can't deal. I'm out of here." Daniel slammed the door.

"What just happened?" Tom asked.

"Do you know what that was about?" I asked Hannah.

"He's been stressed out lately."

"What about?"

"You, school, his girlfriend. Mostly the thought of losing his Mom, his biggest fan," Hannah said.

"Girlfriend? What girlfriend?" I asked.

"Never mind, Mom."

"Where did that come from? Doesn't he know I'm dying? It seems awfully selfish that he can't support me. What could possibly be going on in his life that is as difficult as mine? I'm really blown away. What do you make of that, Tom?"

"He sounds like he's angry and confused. Do you know where he might have gone, Hannah?"

"I'm not sure, but I have an idea. I'll take the car and go look for him."

"Let me come with you."

"No, Mom. He needs some space."

Hannah grabbed my keys and left to find Daniel. Tom and I sat in the living room in disbelief.

"He seems really upset," Tom said.

"Can you believe he is blaming me for his problems? I'm just trying to stay alive."

I gestured at my power chair and threw my hands in the air.

"I don't know, honey. I've got some work to do tonight."

Tom got up and went into his office and shut the door. I did not want to be left alone. I've always been there for Daniel, never missed a teacher conference or football game. Maybe that was my mistake, always putting my family first and not taking care of myself. It was all I could do to get out of bed today. What more does he want from me? I picked up a stack of paperwork and started reading about the stem cell trial. Hannah returned an hour later.

"Hi, honey," I yelled from the living room. "Did you find him?"

Hannah walked into the living room.

"No. I looked in all the typical places and couldn't find him."

"Did you call his friends?"

"I texted everyone, including Daniel."

"I'm worried sick," I said.

"I'm going to go make supper. There's nothing more I can do for now," Hannah said.

Grief overwhelmed me, isolation my only friend. My health, and now my family, were crashing down around me. The Janene of old would put on a happy face and persevere, hoping things would eventually get better. That was no longer working for me. I needed a new way of doing things and a new way of being. But how? I didn't have a clue. I rolled into the kitchen to see if there was anything I can do to help Hannah with supper.

"Thanks for looking for your brother."

"No worries. I know he'll show up eventually; he just needs some time alone to think," Hannah said.

"Anything I can do to help with supper?"

"No. I'm just throwing a salad together. Is Dad home?"

"Yes, he's in his office working."

"You can tell Dad that supper is ready."

I rolled to Tom's office. "Are you hungry? Supper is ready."

"Yes. Did the kids make it home?"

"Hannah is home and made a salad for us. No sign of Daniel."

"That kid," Tom said. I followed Tom into the kitchen. "Thanks for making supper."

"I wish I could have found Daniel tonight," Hannah said.

"I'm sure he'll show up soon," Tom said.

I poked at my salad with a fork held by withered hands. I choked on a piece of lettuce the last time I had eaten a salad. So this time, I picked out the chicken and cut it into petite bites, leaving the lettuce behind. It came to mind that I have been modifying my eating habits, avoiding dry foods like chips and nuts. Even my favorite protein bars had been set aside. My new culinary delights included yogurt, noodles, and mashed potatoes.

I was exhausted and couldn't wait to get to bed. Lying in bed, I felt normal as long as I didn't try to move. But, sleep would not come to me until Daniel was home.

"I'd like to go to bed early tonight. Can you help me to bed, Tom?"

"I doubt you will be able to sleep."

"That's for sure. But, I'll feel better in bed rather than in my wheelchair."

So began the longest night, yearning to toss and turn, but my legs refused. I felt like I was free-falling down a black hole. When will I hit bottom? Will a parachute deploy to save me? Exhale. I startled at the sound of Tom's phone. I glanced at the bedside clock, 3:34 am. Tom groaned, put on his glasses, and fumbled his cellphone.

"Hello. Yes, this is Tom Branch, Daniel's father."

"Who is it?" I asked.

Tom pointed his finger and shushed me.

"Excuse me?" Tom said. "What did Daniel do?"

"What? What happened?"

"Okay, officer, I'm on my way." Tom grabbed his jeans and shirt and headed to the bathroom.

"What the hell is going on?" I said, competing with the sound of Tom's pee hitting the toilet water. "Is Daniel okay?"

"He's in the hospital," Tom said as he grabbed his ball cap and phone.

"Wait! You can't leave me here!"

"I've got to go," Tom said.

The nerve. How could he leave me here, stuck in bed? I beat

my comforter with balled fists and yelled for Hannah.

"I'm coming, Mom." Half asleep, Hannah walked into my bedroom. "What's going on?"

"Daniel is in the hospital!"

"What? What happened?"

"I have no idea. Dad got a phone call, and he left me here, stuck."

"Oh, God. I hope he's okay."

"He's got to be okay. Please help me get dressed and into my wheelchair."

"Let me throw some clothes on first," Hannah said.

Hannah got me dressed and into the van in record time. I had a new appreciation for our accessible van. The side ramp is the easiest and safest way to get me in and out. But, dear God, it was expensive. The conversion cost more than the van itself.

We drove to the hospital in a hurry. The parking fairy was with us; an accessible van spot was open. My novice power chair driving skills appeared as I tried to exit the van in a hurry. I rammed into the back seat several times and got stuck.

"Take it easy, Mom."

"I wish I could drive this thing," I said.

"You've got this. Take your time."

"All I've got is a kid in the hospital, and I don't know why."

I rammed my chair a few more times and broke free from my self imposed jam. We entered the bright lights of the emergency room and inquired at the reception desk.

"I'm looking for my son, Daniel Branch," I said.

The rotund security guard pecked at his keyboard without looking up.

"Identification?"

Hannah handed the guard her driver's license from her wallet.

"What about her?" the guard said as he looked in my direction.

"Did you bring your purse?" Hannah asked.

"No. We left in such a hurry."

"What's her name?" he asked Hannah.

"Janene Branch," Hannah and I said in unison.

Seriously? I didn't have time to school him on the fact that there is no correlation between leg function and brain function. I thought he would know better working in a hospital where wheelchairs abound.

"Spell that," he said without looking up from the monitor.

"J-a-n-e-n-e," I said before Hannah could answer.

The guard handed Hannah our temporary ID badges and remotely opened the doors to the emergency room. "Check-in at the nurses' station through the double doors."

The automatic doors parted, and we approached the nurses' station.

"I'm looking for my son, Daniel Branch."

"He's in room 3A, up ahead on your right," the nurse said.

"Thank you."

The ER was eerily quiet, nothing like you'd see on TV. Daniel appeared to be asleep in the hospital bed with Tom at his side.

"Oh my God, what happened?" I asked as I rolled next to the bedside and picked up Daniel's hand. It appeared lifeless yet felt warm.

"The cops found him passed out in the park," Tom said. "Oxycodone overdose."

My mouth opened to speak, but no words came. It's not possible. Not my Daniel. I couldn't see clearly.

"Someone made an anonymous call to 911, saying a teenage boy was passed out in the park," Tom said. "The police who arrived at the scene first saved his life."

"Oxycodone? No way. Why do they think it was Oxy?" I asked.

"They found your prescription bottle in his pocket."

I looked down.

"Is he going to be okay?"

"The doctor isn't sure. We don't know how long he was unconscious. We have to wait and see what happens," Tom said.

Daniel's chest heaved, and vomit flew out of his mouth, asphyxiating him.

"Hannah, get the nurse quick!" Tom said. Hannah ran out of the room and returned with the doctor and a team of nurses.

"Get the family out, we need room to work here," the doctor said.

A flurry of activity pushed us outside of the treatment room. Not being able to help my child left me feeling more helpless than ALS did. We were escorted to a small waiting room. A nice guy gave me a towel to wipe Daniel's vomit off my shirt, hands, and face. I'd just realized that the stomach acid burned my exposed skin. Hannah came to me to help clean me off.

"Did you know anything about this?"

"No, Mom. I knew he was having a hard time, but I had no idea about this."

"It's probably the new girlfriend. Do you know who she is?"

"I don't know her well. But I doubt it's her. Why are you looking to blame someone, Mom? Let's focus our energy on Daniel coming out of this okay."

About 20 minutes later, the doctor came in. "It looks like Daniel is going to come out of this. He aspirated on some of his stomach contents, so we're going to have to watch for pneumonia. But, he is breathing on his own, and that's a good sign."

"When can we take him home?"

"We are going to keep him for a few days for observation."

"Can we go see him now?"

"Yes. Keep visitors and interruptions to a minimum. He needs to rest."

I walked into Daniel's hospital room to the sounds and lights of monitors. He looked broken and helpless like Hell had washed over him. He appeared to be asleep, so I sat beside him and wondered where I had gone wrong, how had I failed him. He awoke and turned his head toward me. His sandy blond hair hung over his eyes. I longed to cradle him as I did when he was a boy in need of his mother. I had become a source of pain, rather than comfort.

"Hi, son. You're going to be okay." I combed the hair away

from his eyes with my fingers.

"Sorry, Mom."

"I wish I could take all this mess away. I feel awful that I'm causing you so much pain."

"Not everything is about you. Can't you just get over yourself." Daniel closed his eyes and turned his head away. An ache rolled through me. Another disappointment to tuck into my parcel of despair.

Daniel was ready to go home two days later. Tom wanted to handle Daniel's discharge. He said I'm not emotionally stable enough to deal with it. Thank you, Captain Obvious. With Daniel on the road to recovery, I called Dallas to let her know I was ready to start the stem cell trial.

"Hi, Dallas. This is Janene Branch. I'm ready to go; when can we get started?" I said in a voicemail.

I checked into the hospital two months later for the first stem cell treatment of the clinical trial. Having Hannah with me calmed my nerves. She seemed confident and always knew what was best. During the first treatment, Dr. Winters injected millions of stem cells into my spinal column. No one was sure how it worked. Regardless, we hoped the stem cells would support my motor neurons that were dying in droves. I was under anesthesia during treatment, so naturally, I don't remember a thing. When I awoke from surgery, I was cold and sore. But overall, I felt pretty good.

Dallas came to see me the next morning, bringing a cup of real coffee for me. She asked me 20 questions about how I was feeling. Dr. Winters came to see me that afternoon and performed a routine neurological exam. He told me my blood work looked good. And as far as he could tell, I was doing well after the first treatment.

Hannah and I stayed in the hospital for four more days of observation. I don't know if it was a placebo effect or actual benefit from the treatment, but I felt stronger and more coordinated by the day. Dr. Winters said it is too early to tell why I was feeling so well. But I'd take it, placebo or not.

Hannah and I came back a month later for my second treatment. Dallas asked me all the questions on the ALS functional rating scale. Nothing had changed dramatically, but I still felt stronger and more coordinated.

"Things are looking good," Dallas said.

"I'm feeling good," I said. "I'm hoping to feel even better after this treatment."

"We are only looking at the safety during the phase 1 part of this trial. But of course, we are all delighted that you are feeling well."

Hannah was at my bedside when I awoke from surgery. "How are you feeling, Mom?"

"The anesthesia makes me nauseous. But other than that, I'm okay."

Dallas and Dr. Winters joined me in the recovery room.

"How's my star patient doing?" Dr. Winters asked.

"I'm feeling good considering you were just all up inside my spinal column."

"Always the jokester, you are," Dallas said.

"I won't be joking when I walk out of here on Friday."

"Well, now it's time for some rest. I'll come by in the morning with coffee and a needle for another blood draw," Dallas said.

Friday morning came in a hurry, and I was feeling fantastic. Dr. Winters came in for a final exam and to discharge me from the hospital.

"Hey Doc, watch this," I said as I stood up from my wheelchair, supported only by a walker in front of me.

"Impressive. Look at you," Dr. Winters said. "Be careful."

"I am unstoppable. I can't wait for the next treatment."

"We will have to wait until next month," Dr. Winters said.

"I'll see you then."

I continued to feel stronger and more capable over the next few weeks. My wheelchair gathered dust in the corner as I walked around the house using only a walker or cane. I felt on top of the world. I knew for sure that I was in the treatment group and not getting a placebo. The next treatment continued with the same great results. I was distressed that the trial came to an end after only four treatments.

"Let's go over the ALS functional rating scale again," Dallas said. "I see that you can walk again. Are you able to climb stairs?"

"I can get up the stairs, but I still need a little help from behind."

"What about self-care, can you dress?"

"I can, but I need a little help in the shower." We finished the questions and reviewed my blood work.

"Have you noticed any adverse events since the last treatment?"

"Well, I may have gained a few pounds since it's easier to get to the refrigerator now," I said. "And the walking thing, I'd put that in the win column."

"Unfortunately, we are only assessing safety in this trial," Dallas said.

Dr. Winters joined us and asked, "How are you feeling, Janene?"

"Never better."

"Your blood work looks great, and it looks like you've gained two points on the functional rating scale. That is unusual."

"Can I continue the treatments even though this part of the trial is over?"

"I'm sorry, no. We can't offer treatment until we get FDA approval. And even that is a long shot and will take years."

"I don't have years to wait for the FDA."

"I understand the urgency. I've had hundreds of patients die from this horrific disease. I appreciate your sacrifices and willingness to participate in this trial. So far, the safety profile is impressive. "

"Is it really over?" I asked.

"The treatments are complete, but you have a follow-up appointment in 30 days."

"See you then," I said.

Daniel and Tom were home when Hannah and I arrived. My back was a little sore, but I managed to walk in the house using only my cane.

"Mom, you're walking!" Daniel said, reaching to hug me.

"Careful, honey. My back is sore."

"Did the stem cells work? Are you going to be okay?" Daniel asked.

"For now, things are looking better. But the trial is over and I won't be getting any more treatments. Enough about me. It's so great to see you. How are you doing?"

"I'm not going to lie, I've been worried. But I'm handling it. I promise."

"I'm very proud of you."

"Thanks, Mom. I'm proud of you too."

I went back to see Dr. Winters the following month. "How are you doing, Janene?"

"My legs are getting weaker. I'm afraid I'm losing some of the gains I've made."

"That's disappointing to hear, but not unusual," Dr. Winters said.

"I've gone from ecstatic to very concerned in just a month. You have to find a way to keep giving me treatments."

"I wish that were possible. But, there is no way."

"It's so unfair. How can this happen? I went from dying, to walking again, and back to dying. There has got to be someone you can call or something you can do."

"I'm so sorry, Janene. The FDA regulations won't allow it. We will just have to wait and see how you progress."

CHAPTER ELEVEN

Cora

Westbrook, North Carolina
Spring, 1889

My story is a freedom song of struggle. It is about
finding one's purpose, how to overcome fear, and
to stand up for causes bigger than one's self.
– Coretta Scott King

Eli returned to Westbrook to check on a lumber order for the Vanderbilt house. He never failed to stop by to pay his respects to Hattie and to fill up on a home-cooked meal.

"I sure do miss your cooking, Mama," Eli said when he came home on one of his visits.

"I sure miss seeing your face. Don't you eat over there in Asheville?"

"I've been eating well since I got hired on at the Biltmore project. We are building the biggest house you've ever laid eyes on. It will have over 200 rooms. Can you imagine that?"

"That's big enough to house all the orphans," I said.

"Sure enough. We already built an entire village for the workers. They are expecting 1,000 men. There's a kiln to make bricks right there. I've been working in the woodshop for now, but have hopes of working with the limestone craftsman. They sure have a way with stone."

"Sounds like you're busy," I said.

"I'll be a master builder when I'm done."

Eli puffed his chest like a tom on the hunt for a hen. I could forget Eli when he wasn't around. But, when he came home my heart fluttered like a butterfly in the spring, searching for a place to land yet too fearful to trust a safe landing. A sharp inhale and a pain in my chest reminded me that I didn't deserve that kind of love, destined to never marry.

"Looks like you've got a house full of young ones here," Eli said.

"Well, about that. I've been praying about something. I want to open an orphanage for Negro children," I said.

"How is that any different than what we have here now? We take care of the children we have, feed them, love them, give them a warm bed at night. We teach them to read and write too. Isn't that enough?" Hattie said.

"Plenty enough. I've been reading about opening an official orphanage with the state of North Carolina. That way, we can help even more children, and we also can get money from the state, churches, or other organizations to help pay for things."

Hattie gave me that look of hers. That look meant that she didn't think it was a good idea.

"You keep praying on that," Hattie said. "I don't want strangers in our business."

My heart sank. I was hoping Hattie would be open to the idea. I knew I had some convincing to do.

Eli broke the uncomfortable silence. "Thanks for dinner, Mama. Got any work I can do around the house today before I head back to Asheville in the morning?"

"Chop up some of that firewood this evening and stack it next to the shed."

"Yes, ma'am. I wish I had some of the fancy saws with me from Asheville. It would cut the work in half."

"Go on, you and your fancy saws," Hattie said.

Eli went outside to tend to the firewood while I cleaned the dishes. I blushed when Hattie caught me watching Eli through the window.

"He's been gone 15 years, and you still can't get that man off your mind."

"Excuse me, Mama, I've got some reading to do in my room."

"I hope you're reading the Bible," Hattie said.

I opened my Bible, but not to read God's word. I opened my Bible and pulled out a newspaper clipping from the Oxford Daily Ledger, crisp folds and torn edges, still white as it had been kept in the dark. "Local churches provide funding for the state's first orphanage for Negro children." The article went on to say, "Without the safety of slave owners, many Negro children are left to fend for themselves. Without an orphanage, the Negro children are dirty and often steal just to survive. It is for the betterment of our town and the betterment of Negro children that we provide a safe home for them."

I longed to go to Oxford to see the orphanage for myself. I pictured children laughing and playing, healthy with clean clothes and full stomachs. What if I borrowed a horse? It would take me weeks to get there, but I could see it for myself. I was just fooling myself. No way Mama would let me, a lone Negro woman, go all that distance. She'd call it pure foolishness. I put my dream back in my Bible and saved it for another day.

I enjoyed my morning coffee on the back porch, a rare treat considering all the young ones living with us. A red cardinal swooped in, displacing the peaceful goldfinches perched on the fence. The startled goldfinches reminded me that there is someone more significant, more aggressive than me, wanting to knock me off my perch. Granted, I no longer cowed to the plantation overseer, yet I remained captive, as an unmarried Negro woman, to society's beliefs about my worth.

I heard unfamiliar footsteps and the telling creak of the old porch wood.

"New boots?" I asked without looking up.

"Yes, new work boots for the master craftsman," Eli said.

"May I join you this lovely morning, Miss Cora?"

"I won't stop you."

"It's always nice to see you when I come home. I reckoned you'd be married off by now," Eli said.

"I told you that's not going to happen, remember?"

"Yes, but someone as pretty as you? It would be a miracle to see you as an old maid."

"I believe in miracles. Eli, how far is it from your work in Ashville to Oxford?"

"Oxford?" Eli asked.

"That's where they opened that orphanage for Negro children, like the one I want to open here in Westbrook."

"I don't know where Oxford is, but I can ask around when I get back to Asheville."

"Much obliged, Eli. It's important to me, the orphanage."

I waved goodbye to Eli as he mounted his horse, heading east to Asheville. My hands folded on my chest as I exhaled, my gaze landed on Eli's broad shoulders and muscles that rippled through his shirt. Jesus would not approve of my thoughts.

"Help me get the children ready, Cora," Hattie said from the porch, bringing me back to reality.

"Coming, Mama."

I went inside and tended to the children, grateful for the distraction.

"Wash your hands and face in the basin, all you fine, young men. Come along, young ladies, let's give the boys some room."

"Time for breakfast, young ones," Hattie said.

"Coming, Mama Hattie," the children said in unison as they scrambled to the table.

"Lizbeth, say the blessing."

"Yes, Mama Hattie."

Lizbeth, a sweet girl from Rutherford County, came to us last month after her mama died from the winter fever.

"Thank you, Lord, for this meal before us and bless the hands that made it. Amen."

"Amen."

I smiled as the sound of chattering children and forks on tin plates filled the room, comforting as the smell of baking bread.

"Do we have enough food to get us through the week?"

"Eli left us enough money to get by for a few weeks."

"Should I look for a job? I can bring some money to help raise the children."

"I need you here, Cora, to help with the children."

"Yes, Mama."

Sleep didn't come easily that night as I thought about how to take care of the children. Like Jacob, I wrestled all night with an angel. Unlike Jacob, I didn't have a broken hip, and I didn't have to change my name to Israel when I woke up, yet I had to overcome my fear and find a way. Hattie won't be around forever, and her work must continue. I must get my head straight.

"God, if you're there, make a way. There's got to be a way."

After hours of staring at the ceiling in the dark, I got up to boil water for the weekly washing, scrubbed the children's clothes, and hung them on the line by the first light of sunrise. The lye soap left a gray film in the cracks of my hands, drawing notice to years of labor. I gathered eggs and made biscuits before the children stirred.

I put fresh warm water in the basin and cleaned myself up as best I could. I felt my braids, loose, maybe Meriday can tighten them next week. I looked at the bottom of my cedar chest, a gift from Eli, for a presentable wrapper and rag to cover my messy braids. I found the blue dress Hattie gave me the day Eli and Lewis found me under the tree. I'd filled out some, so the dress fit.

"I've got a few errands to run, Mama. I'll be back soon," I said, scurrying out of the house before Hattie could stop me.

I stepped onto the street, jutted my chin, straightened my dress, and walked straight toward my dreams coming true.

I walked to the dry goods store to order some thread and three new needles. We had just finished teaching the girls how to weave homespun, and now we had enough fabric to sew some clothing for the children. While in town, I decided to take the first step. The Westbrook church stood just a few blocks away.

Standing in front of two wooden doors, I exhaled and pressed my knees together to keep them from shaking. I'd never stepped foot in a white church before and feared what could happen. I knocked on the door and listened, nothing. I tried again, still nothing. I walked away, defeated. No. I turned on my heel and walked back to the church doors. Hands shaking, I reached up and pulled the black metal handle, and the door opened. I stepped inside.

"Hello, anyone here?"

Dust floated in the rays of light. The smell of old wood hit my nose.

An older, white woman approached me. "Hello, dear. How may I help you?"

"Good morning, ma'am. My name is Cora, daughter of Miss Hattie."

"Pleasure to meet you, Miss Cora. My name is Ada, I'm the caretaker. Please come in. Can I get you a cup of tea?"

"No, thank you, ma'am."

I looked down to avoid making eye contact. I found it interesting that this woman, who treated me kindly, had the same name as my mama.

"I come seeking charity for Negro orphans. You see, Hattie and I take in children who have nowhere to go and no place to call home. Her sons are grown and gone now, so it's hard. Sorry to be a bother, ma'am."

"No bother at all, Cora. Yours is a lovely idea. Please come back on Tuesday evening at six sharp. That's when the deacons meet, and you can make your request directly."

"Much obliged, Miss Ada. Thank you kindly."

I gathered myself and headed home. I had two days to explain all of this to Hattie. Did she need to know? Maybe I won't tell her anything at all.

Tuesday evening came, and fear nearly froze me in place. My desire to continue Hattie's work gave me the strength needed. I reached for my necklace, still there. Breathe. I opened the door and stepped inside a white church for the second time.

"Good evening, Miss Cora," Ada said. "The deacons are expecting you."

"Good evening, ma'am."

"Follow me."

I followed Ada into the sanctuary. It smelled of oiled wood and candles, fancier than any church I'd ever seen. I looked toward the front of the room and saw two rows of mostly gray-haired men. They were laughing and appeared to be catching up on the news of the week.

"Pardon me, Deacon Ashby," Ada said. "This is Hattie's daughter, Cora. She has a request."

"Welcome, Cora. We don't see a lot of Negros here at Westbrook Church," Deacon Ashby said.

"Hear, hear," echoed a chorus of deacons.

"Yes, sir. The colored church doesn't have any money to help the orphans, and because we serve the same God, I thought maybe the fine folk here at Westbrook Church could help."

"Deacon Ashby, I'd like to hear more details," a short, round man said.

"Yes, Brother Horton. I agree," Deacon Ashby said.

Brother Horton, a short, round man. A short, round man. I looked at him and felt dizzy.

"What's the matter? Cat got your tongue?" Brother Horton said.

He reared his head back and laughed, exposing his rotten and missing teeth. Oh, my Lord. It's him. I stumbled and caught myself on a pew. I couldn't get air into my lungs, I felt like someone or something pushed down on my head. I heard myself groan as I slumped to the ground.

I awoke on my back with my head cradled in Miss Ada's lap. A cold rag soothed my forehead.

"Wake up, Cora. Dear Cora," Ada said.

I sat up, straightened my dress, and accepted the cup of water from Deacon Ashby.

"Thank you, Deacon," I said as I took a sip of water. "I'm sorry.

I didn't mean to cause trouble."

"You're no trouble, dear," Ada said. "Are you able to get up?"

"Yes, ma'am."

I stood up, shaken but not deterred. I couldn't run, I needed their help. How? I reached for my necklace and heard my mother say, "You were born for something more, you're going to be somebody. Your story is important." That's it. I'll tell them my story.

"I'm sorry about that. Please let me share my story with you so you can see how important Miss Hattie's work is."

I looked to Deacon Ashby and he nodded his head.

"When I was a child, I lived on the Yarbrough Plantation with my mama, daddy, and two little brothers, Samuel and Abner."

I took a deep breath to calm my nerves and shaking hands. I'd never talked about this before, never spoken a word.

"One day, the worst day of my life, three men attacked my family. I saw them beat my daddy. Then they shot him and my brothers too. They died, right there in the field."

Smug looks and smiles left the men's faces. Some looked at their boots, others scratched their beards. I watched brother Horton as he ran his hand over his bald, greasy head. Did he know I was talking about him? I stared at him, my tears welling, voice shaking.

"Then they attacked my mama and me." Tears spilled onto my cheeks, through clenched teeth I said, "They did to Mama and me, what I can't say aloud, especially here in the Lord's house. Then, they shot Mama, and I ran."

The room fell silent as I turned my back to wipe my tears and take a drink of water. The cup shook in my hands, and water spilled down my dress. I turned back around and continued.

"Hattie's sons found me, my dress bloody and torn, and they took me to Hattie. I've been there to this day. Hattie saved my life and I want to help other children as she helped me. We need five dollars a week to take care of the children. Please help us."

"Five dollars a week? That is a poor man's fortune," Deacon Ashby said.

"Hear, hear!"

"If I may," Brother Horton said. "Let's consider how the fine town of Westbrook can benefit. Having an orphanage will keep the young Negros off the streets, begging as they do."

Brother Horton nodded at me, framed with a nervous smile as though he begged forgiveness as if the money atoned for his sins.

"Brother Horton, you know, we don't have that much money in our coffers," Deacon Ashby said.

"I will personally assure the coffers remain adequately supplied," Brother Horton said.

"Well, I can't argue with that," Deacon Ashby said. "Cora, you and Hattie have our pledge of support."

"Much obliged, sir. Thank you all," I said with my head bowed.

I looked at Brother Horton until his eyes met mine in agreement. He had bought my silence, for now.

CHAPTER TWELVE

Amadahy

Aguaquiri
Flower Moon, 1664

Where there is love, there is life.
– Mahatma Gandhi

I recognized Quatsey from behind as we approached the group of women who were processing the new bounty of cane. Our escort signaled us to stop.

"Quatsey, you have visitors from the north."

Quatsey stood and turned toward us. I gasped, stunned by her beauty.

"We met at the river. What a surprise to see you here. Welcome," Quatsey said.

"We traveled today to find you because we need your help."

"Excuse me, I need to show hospitality to my guest." Quatsey walked toward us. "Let's talk privately. Come with me."

"Thank you for showing us kindness," I said to the men.

Leotie and I followed Quatsey to her home. It looked much like our home, a hearth in the middle for cooking and warmth, dirt floors. The startling difference was the woven masterpieces adorning her home. Baskets of vegetables and woven mats displayed her handicraft.

"Your home is beautiful, your basket and mats," I said.

"Thank you, I enjoy weaving very much. May I offer you something to eat?"

"That would be nice, thank you."

"We lost our provisions to a hungry bear on our journey. But, that's a story for another time," Leotie said.

"That must be a story to tell," Quatsey said as she served us rabbit stew that was simmering on the fire.

"What brings you all this way?"

"I must say, I was impressed with the weaving on your mat. The one that carried your river cane. It's like nothing I've seen before. Would you be willing to teach Leotie and me how to weave like you?"

"Look at this basket. You see how desperate we are," Leotie said.

"Uwata," Quatsey said.

We laughed with the comfort of old friends as if our spirits had connected in the lavender meadow.

"No one in our village has your skill or talent," I said.

"I'd love to share my gift with you. What kind of weaving do you want to do?"

"Basic household baskets and mats to start. I would like to weave small boxes for storing dried flowers, resins, and herbs for both Gawonii, our medicine man, and for myself."

"The medicine man? Is this a love interest?"

"No, just a friend."

"Gowanii helped my twin Ahyoka and me when we had the fever," Leotie said.

"Where's Ahyoka now?"

"She is buried in the side of the mountain with my great grandmother," Leotie said.

"I'm sad to hear about your sister. It must be hard for the whole family, especially you, Leotie."

"It's just my mom and me. Well, Grandma lives with us. But she has a mean spirit living in her."

Quatsey looked to me, I shrugged and said, "Children speak

the truth."

"Eat and rest from your journey, then we can join the others in preparing the cane."

We finished our stew and rested briefly. I was excited to meet the other villagers and to get started weaving so we didn't pause for long. We walked back to the village center to join the women.

The village was similar to mine but with a thicker canopy of trees. Well worn footpaths led to the village center like a medicine circle. The women appeared similar in dress wearing deerskin wraps with a noticeable difference, they grew taller and more muscular than the women of my village to the north. The women hushed their conversation as we approached the circle. Either Quatsey led the women, and they showed her respect, or we were the topic of their conversation.

"You have made good progress," Quatsey said to the women.

"We cut and scrape in much the same way. Do you use bloodroot and black walnut to dye the cane?" I asked.

"Yes, I stored the walnut husks we harvested during the nut moon and the dried bloodroot we harvested during the ripe corn moon. Do you want to help me pound the roots, Leotie?" Quatsey asked.

"Yes, I would like that. Can we do it together?" Leotie looked down and fingered the fringe on her dress. "I like you."

My heart melted as Quatsey embraced Leotie and said, "I like you too."

I liked Quatsey too. She moved with grace and confidence, blending in like an animal on the hunt, and yet reflecting the glory of the sun. I would follow her anywhere.

"Let's get started," Quatsey said as she grabbed the baskets of husks and roots and walked to the community grinding stones. Generations of women milled bowl-shaped impressions into the large rocks. Baskets of corn by the thousands, ground by women sharing their lives, encouraging one another, and gossiping about others.

"The husks make less of a mess, so we will start with them,"

Quatsey said as she put husks on the stones in front of us. We each picked up a grinder stone and began our journey together as weavers.

"Is your family here in the village with you?" I asked.

"My mother and grandmother were warriors and were killed in an attack by men with pale skin."

"That's terrible. I'm so sorry."

"I was very young. I don't have many memories of my mother," Quatsey said.

I remembered the elders spoke of the tension between the Cherokee and Shawnee. Our chief allowed Shawnee refugees to settle nearby when they retreated from the Iroquois. Then, the Shawnee people moved into our land and attacked hunting parties and made away with the bounty. Our warriors retaliated by attacking in small bands and scattering in different directions afterward, making it easier to escape.

"Your mother, an ayastigi, your grandmother, a warrior too. Was it the Shawnee?"

"Yes. Their horses were injured during an attack, and they were unable to get away on foot," Quatsey said as she stared to the east. "The Shawnee hunted them, an arrow in my mother's back, and an arrow in my grandmother's neck. Senseless violence, I'll never understand."

"How do you keep your mother's memory alive?" Leotie asked.

"I think about her every day. Let me show you something."

Quatsey walked to the northwest corner of the house and pulled out a square basket from under a neatly stacked pile of skins.

"My mother wore this when she went into battle." Quatsey unfolded a leather bodice like she was unwrapping a newborn child. "Look at the colorful beads of corn and dried berries." She ran her fingers over the beadwork. "These are the claws, bones, and teeth of animals that provided food for our family."

"It's beautiful. You honor your mother."

"What's that?" Leotie asked, pointing to the square basket.

"That necklace."

"That was my grandmother's. She said she would give it to me when the time was right. It's an interesting charm."

Quatsey picked up the necklace and rubbed her thumb over the bone carving.

"My great grandmother had the same necklace. You should wear it."

Quatsey handed the necklace to Leotie. "Help me put it on."

"Do you have any brothers or sisters?" Leotie asked.

"I have two older brothers that raised me. They both married women in the Long Hair Clan to the south. So, I live alone now."

"Do you get lonely living all by yourself?"

"Sometimes. But, I've always been a free spirit, not following the traditions of our foremothers. I guess that's what happens when you're raised by boys."

"Well, I think you are beautiful," Leotie said.

"Why, thank you, Leotie. You are quite the young woman."

We giggled at Leotie's innocence. Leotie had the strength to say what I was thinking.

"Tell me about your sister," Quatsey asked.

"Thanks for asking. I like to talk about my sister and to honor her memory. She had an adventurous spirit, I think she was a white rabbit."

"My two girls, together, always found mischief. I didn't think I would miss that part, but I do," I said.

"That sounds like me when I was a young girl," Quatsey said.

We finished grinding the walnut husks.

"My work goes faster with three of us working together. Leotie, go to my house, and get the two biggest pots you can find," Quatsey said.

"For boiling the bloodroot and walnut?"

"Yes, Leotie."

When Leotie left Quatsey turned to me and said, "She is wise for her young years."

"Sometimes, she is wiser than me."

"Amadahy, would you consider staying with me while I teach

you my weaving technique? It will take some time. I would also like to learn about healing plants from you."

"That is very generous of you. I would like that very much."

Leotie returned with the pots, and we emptied our baskets of ground walnut husks.

"We will simmer the husks with water when the sun goes down. Pounding the bloodroot can make a terrible mess. Try not to get it on your clothes," Quatsey said.

"Pounding bloodroot is good for releasing frustration. Rather than being angry at my mother or ex-husband, I see their faces instead of the root," I said.

"Mama, that's a terrible thought."

"That can be very practical," Quatsey said.

A young woman approached us and spoke to Quatsey. "The women are done cutting cane for the day. We will begin again tomorrow when we are finished with our morning work."

"Thank you," Quatsey said.

"Let's save the bloodroot for tomorrow. We've accomplished a lot for one day."

We gathered our supplies and returned to Quatsey's home. We put the baskets and pots near the hearth and prepared the evening meal, steamed greens and dried bear meat. A feast by most standards.

"Did I hear you say something about an ex-husband?" Quatsey asked as her arm brushed against mine. I felt a tingle run down the length of my back, fine hairs stood tall on my arm.

"Waya, of the Long Hair Clan. Maybe your brothers know of him. We married because the girls grew in my womb, not because we loved each other. It wasn't meant to be. He returned to his clan while the twins lay ill. Do you have a husband?"

"No. I've had men who showed interest, but none of them turned my head or gave me a reason to pause."

I wondered if I had caused her head to turn. Was Quatsey a two-spirit, transcending traditional gender roles? My mind opened to loving a woman. It set well with my spirit, yet foreign to my thinking. I liked the idea of being in love, real love, not love from a sense of duty. Was I foolish to entertain such fantasy? Quatsey declared herself a free spirit. Free indeed.

"We should bring the canoe in from the riverbank before darkness comes," I said. "Let's go, Leotie."

"I'll stay here and boil the walnut husks," Quatsey said.

Leotie and I retraced the path we walked earlier that day. We found our canoe where we left it by the riverbank and carried it back without incident.

"Bring the last basket inside with you."

"Yes, Mother." Leotie reached into the canoe for the basket and screamed like an injured wildcat. "Ow! Mama! Something got my hand."

I ran to see what happened. "My hand, my hand."

I looked at her hand, two small holes marked her first finger. Quatsey ran to us when she heard the screams.

"What happened?" Quatsey asked.

"Snakebite."

I moved Leotie away from the canoe to avoid a second attack.

"It hurts so much, Mama."

"I know, I know it does. Let's go inside and sit down. Take a deep breath to calm yourself. Quatsey, take a careful look in the canoe and see if you can find the snake. I need to know what kind. I saw a flash of red, I fear it might be a copperhead."

I held Leotie's injured hand up to my chest as we walked inside. Why didn't I get the basket myself? I would have tended to my own wound.

Quatsey walked inside. "You're right, Amadahy, it was a copperhead, but it won't bite anyone else."

"Thank you. Do you have my basket? I need lavender and echinacea."

"Yes," Quatsey said as she handed me the basket. "What else can I bring you?"

"I need strips of clean hemp cloth and hot water for tea and the cloth. I'm going to wrap Leotie's hand with lavender and echinacea to bring down the swelling. Look how swollen her hand is already."

"Hurry, Mama."

"I'm going as fast as I can. Lay down and stay calm."

"Here's the bowl of hot water and cloth," Quatsey said.

I made a poultice and wrapped Leotie's hand and laid it on her chest.

"What now?"

"We wait, hoping that her breathing stays strong through the night."

I changed the dressing throughout the night. The swelling reached her elbow, tender and dark. Quatsey took over when I fell asleep. It was the longest night. How could I go on if I lost my second child in as many moons?

The sun shone through the eastern window and onto Leotie. She half-woke and called for me.

"I'm here. Mama's here."

"Ahyoka, she came to see me in my dream."

"How wonderful to see her again." I brushed her hair back, reminding me of when she had the fever.

"She reached her hand out to me, and when I reached for her, she disappeared," Leotie said with fresh tears on her cheeks. Her head fell to the side, and she fell back asleep.

"Is she going to be alright?" Quatsey asked.

"I don't know yet. It's a good sign Leotie made it through the night. We have to keep treating the bite and giving her tea. When she can sit up, I'll give her echinacea root to chew on. I'll smudge the air with sage and echinacea while we wait for healing."

"I'll find some women to pound the bloodroot so you can be here with Leotie," Quatsey said as she placed her hand on my shoulder, bringing me comfort with a single touch. Quatsey returned with a pot of pounded bloodroot, ready for the hearth. We were one step closer to weaving.

"How is Leotie doing?"

"She's been asleep most of the morning. Let's have a look at her hand."

"Ow! It hurts," Leotie said.

Her sore, inflamed arm, reminding me of a swollen animal carcass. Thankfully, it didn't smell like one.

"Can you sit up?" I asked as Quatsey and I helped her sit up. "You need tea and something to eat. How are you feeling?"

"My hand hurts like my spirit did when Ahyoka died."

"My spirit is broken, seeing you suffer. You are strong and brave, soon you will be running through a lavender meadow like the fox," I said.

Quatsey brought tea made from echinacea leaves. "Here's your tea and something you will love to eat."

Quatsey gave Leotie a drink of tea and a bite of meat. Leotie wanted more, hungry as a winter wolf.

"What is that you're feeding Leotie?"

A mischievous grin grew across Quatsey's face as she said, "It's the meat of a certain copperhead snake."

Leotie spit out a mouthful of chewed snake in surprise. The three of us laughed until Leotie forgot her pain.

CHAPTER THIRTEEN

Janene

Westbrook, North Carolina
2015

Tears are the silent language of grief.
– Voltaire

The last ten months were brutal, like the stem cell treatments never happened. My body atrophied to unrecognizable skin and bones with a bloated belly. Breathing remained my only independent function during my waking hours. Our bedroom morphed into a hospital room, the furniture replaced by medical equipment and clothing replaced by medical supplies. Technology replaced lost physical function: a patient lift, a hospital bed, a shower chair with a roll-in shower, a minivan with a ramp for my power chair, a speech generation device activated by eye movement, a ventilator, cough assist and suction machines, catheters, a feeding tube, palliative medications, all needed to keep me alive and comfortable.

Hannah decided to take care of me at home rather than leave for college. I felt equal parts of protest and relief. I didn't want to be the reason Hannah delayed college. Yet, if I were to die this year, she is the one I wanted to care for me. This was one of many difficult decisions to be made with a terminal illness.

"Are you ready to get up, Mom?" Hannah asked.

"Please shoot some coffee directly into my feeding tube first," I said, sounding intoxicated as my tongue operated at fifty percent.

"Sure thing. The bright side is now you can drink the cheap stuff. You don't need gourmet coffee in a g-tube," Hannah said as she maneuvered tubes and syringes like a seasoned RN. Sweet Hannah, compassionate, and the eternal optimist began my morning routine without complaint.

"You haven't been getting enough water," Hannah said as she held up a plastic urinal containing a few ounces of dark urine emptied from the catheter bag hanging from my hospital bed. "I'll add more water to your feeding tube routine."

Hannah adjusted the pillows that supported my neck, arms, and legs.

"What's on your agenda today?" I asked.

"I would like to plan another trip to visit Grandma. Maybe Dad and Danny can go too."

"I love the idea, but I couldn't get into Grandma's house."

"I'll talk to Dad and see if we could stay at a hotel nearby. I'm sure there are accessible rooms at the Marriott."

"Let's give it a try. It will be my last vacation."

"Don't say that, Mom. Your crystal ball may be on the fritz."

Tom and I sat on the back porch after dinner as was customary on summer evenings. Sweet tea in hand, Tom covered the end of the straw with his finger and let a few drops of tea into my mouth. The taste of sweet tea flooded my mind with backyard memories of summers raising the kids, picnics, water fights, and laughter. I turned my head toward Tom and used my last ounce of the day's energy to say,

"I love you."

"Love you too, sweetheart. I'm taking vacation time next week, and the four of us are going to spend time with Betty on the coast."

I mustered a grin and blinked both eyes in affirmation.

"The hotel has a beach wheelchair that floats. You won't be

watching from the sidelines this time," Tom said as he reached out and held my lifeless hand.

Saturday morning, Tom and kids loaded me and my equipment into the van, and we headed east. I wondered if this would be my last family vacation or the last time I would see Grandma. With everything I did, significant or mundane, I questioned if it was my last time.

"Buckle up kids, here we go," Tom said.

We backed out of the driveway and headed down Riparian Way as we've done a thousand times before. Yet something was amiss. My stomach felt unsettled, my throat constricted. Tom noticed and asked,

"What's up, honey? You seem worried."

"Just have a bad feeling. But I don't want to put negative energy out there."

"Well, your negative vibe is hitting me upside my head."

"Sorry, honey. I'll try to get it together."

I reclined my power chair and tried to keep my pain and fear from escaping through my tear ducts.

When we arrived in town, Tom and Daniel headed inside to check into the hotel.

"Don't forget the roll-in shower," Hannah said.

"We got it, honey," Dad said.

I watched my two favorite guys walk side-by-side and smiled at the resemblance. The car ride wore me out. Counteracting gravity and the centrifugal force with every bump and turn proved too much for my weak core. A nap ranked first on my agenda. I followed Tom and the kids into the hotel room and rolled into the corner, hoping to stay out of the way. Hannah grabbed a few pillows off of the bed and propped up my swollen feet.

"There you go, Mom."

"Thanks, honey."

"Need anything else?"

"I'm fine." I lied.

"Get some rest, and we will pick up Grandma for dinner,"

Tom said as he kissed me on the forehead.

I burst into tears when Tom left the room. My nose stuffed up and made it hard to breathe. I gasped for air and made a strange honking sound while choking on my mucus. I eventually fell asleep from exhaustion. The next thing I remembered was Hannah bounding into the room.

"Are you ready to go, Mom?"

"I think my pee bag needs emptying first."

Hannah brought the urinal from the bathroom and emptied my urine collection bag.

"How's Grandma doing? "I asked.

"She's moving slower than usual, but she's still spunky Grandma."

"I can't wait to see her."

"She's with Dad and Daniel at the restaurant downstairs."

I followed Hannah into the restaurant and rolled up to the table.

"Hi, Grandma. It's great to see you," I said with my computer-generated voice.

I didn't have enough lung capacity to speak loudly enough to be heard in a restaurant. My lifeless tongue also made it hard to understand me. I compensated by using a speech generation device, a computer I controlled with my eyes. It vocalized what I typed like how Stephen Hawking communicated.

"Oh, Janene, you look like hell," Betty said.

I ignored her.

"What did she say, Tom? I can't understand a thing she is saying," Betty said.

"She said thanks, Grandma. It's been a rough few months for Janene," Tom said.

"It's been a rough few months for all of us," Hannah said.

"I see she is wearing the necklace I gave her."

"She hasn't taken it off since you gave it to her during our last visit."

We enjoyed a quiet dinner and even had enough room to share a few bites of cheesecake.

"I'm tired, Tom. Would you take me home now?" Betty asked.

"Of course. Daniel, will you come with me to take Grandma home?"

"I'll get Mom ready for bed," Hannah said.

Grandma came over for a hug and a kiss good night. "Good night, Janene. I love you."

I blinked and smiled.

The boys left with Grandma, and Hannah followed me to our hotel room.

"What was Grandma whispering to you about?" I typed.

"She was talking to me about the necklace. It sure is an interesting piece."

"Yes, it is," I said.

I felt a strange need to grasp the charm in my hand. I wanted to but the muscles in my arm and hand did not comply. I focused all my energy concentrating on the talisman. I swear, I felt it get hot on my chest. And if I weren't deceived by exhaustion, I would bet what's left of my life that it glowed.

"Are you ready to get into bed?" Hannah asked.

"I'm too tired to transfer into the bed. I'll just recline and sleep in my chair tonight. If you don't mind," I said by reclining and closing my eyes.

"It's up to you, Mom. I'll do whatever makes you happy."

"Sleep will make me happy," I said. Hannah did what she could to make me comfortable. Tom and Daniel returned after a short while.

"Thanks for taking care of Grandma," I said.

"Happy to do it, "Tom said.

"Good night, everyone," I said, hoping my family would take the hint.

I awoke early, anticipating the day at the beach with the family. The sun shone through the crack between the dark hotel curtains. I moved my power chair up and down, hoping the whir of the pneumatics would wake someone else, preferably someone who has access to coffee.

"Good morning, sweetheart. I hear you," Tom said.

"Coffee, please."

"Give me a minute."

The kids roused and shuffled in and out of the bathroom.

"Do you want a shower today?" Hannah asked.

"Yes, that would be wonderful."

Hannah and I danced through our morning routine, made more difficult by a small hotel room.

"Dad, can you help me? I can't maneuver Mom's lift on the carpet."

I swayed back and forth dangling from my patient lift sling. Such a helpless feeling.

"Where are we going?"

"First stop is the toilet," Hannah said.

"Let's roll!" Tom said. I failed to see his humor in the situation.

Thankful to be showered and ready to go, Hannah and I headed to the beach. Tom and Daniel left to get Grandma so she could enjoy a day at the beach with us. I reclined in my accessible beach chair, enjoying the sun.

"Look. Your necklace is reflecting the sun," Hannah said.

"I can feel the warmth. It's weird how the necklace charm heats up when I think about it."

"It's glowing."

I closed my eyes and pondered where life has brought me. Grateful for my marriage and kids. Thankful for my career. Beyond depressed about dying and how painfully difficult the process has been on my family and me. My thoughts shifted to my childhood. Survivor's guilt about living through the accident that killed my family. Lonely. Isolated. Angry my career was taken from me. Infuriated that I'm dying. Anxious because my entire life felt out of control. My breathing became labored, and I panicked.

"Ativan," I mumbled.

"Ativan?"

I blinked my eyes, "Yes."

"It's in the hotel room. Want me to go get it?" Hannah asked.

I blinked again and tried unsuccessfully to calm my breathing. I began choking on mucus. Hannah returned and put the dissolving medication under my tongue.

"Dad and Daniel have been gone a long time," Hannah said. "Maybe, Grandma wasn't ready."

Hannah picked up her phone and started texting. I'd never seen her fingers move so quickly.

"No. No. No," Hannah said.

"What?"

"It can't be." Hannah's chest heaved, eyes wide open, and her mouth agape.

"What? Tell me what's going on!"

Hannah dropped her phone in the sand and said, "Grandma Betty is gone."

My mouth opened, and my anguish fell mute. I closed my eyes, and my talisman burned.

CHAPTER FOURTEEN

Cora

Westbrook, North Carolina
1895

Blessed are those who mourn, for they will be comforted.
– Matthew 5:4

The money from the church came weekly, with no strings attached. Hattie was not pleased, she thought I went behind her back. I got the nerve to tell her about Mr. Horton. I explained how the man who killed my family and did unspeakable things, atoned for his sins by supporting orphans. How fitting, since he made an orphan out of me. "Sweet justice," Hattie called it. Sweet justice, indeed.

"I'll get it." I answered the tapping on the front door. "Hello, may I help you?"

"My name is Mrs. Frederick Scott from Wells Township. I understand you take care of orphan Negros."

Yes, ma'am, we do. Come in, please."

Mrs. Frederick glanced over her shoulder at a horse-drawn wagon, three girls huddled in the back.

"Excuse me, ma'am."

I stepped around Mrs. Frederick and walked towards the girls. I slowed down as I approached the wagon.

"Hi ladies, my name is Cora."

The oldest one, who looked seven, had an arm around each girl and a swaddled infant in her lap, four in all.

Mrs. Frederick approached the wagon. "As I was saying, these children need a home. Their mother died during childbirth a few weeks ago, and their father succumbed to consumption last night."

"Yes, ma'am, much obliged." I returned my attention to the children. "What's your name, child?"

"Selma," the girl with the big, brown eyes said.

"Are these your sisters?"

"Yes, ma'am. Olive and Daisy, they are twins."

"I see that. I also see that you are taking good care of your sisters."

"And my brother, Luther."

"Can I hold him?" I asked with my arms stretched out. Selma handed over the baby, and I gave him a quick look over before I held him close. He appeared lifeless, not enough energy to cry.

"Would you and your sisters like to come inside? We can find something to eat."

"Yes, ma'am. C'mon girls, let's go," Selma said.

The girls climbed off the wagon and waited for me.

"I'll be on my way now," Mrs. Frederick said and turned to the front of the wagon. "Good day."

The lady from Wells Township took the reins and drove away.

"Follow me, girls."

Selma, Olive, and Daisy lined up behind me like ducklings headed to the riverbank. We walked through the house and into the kitchen.

"Have a seat, dear ones."

My thoughts took me back to the first day I sat in this kitchen. I shuddered at the memory of what brought me there. I wondered if Selma felt the same fear, a stranger in a strange place.

"My, my, what do we have here?" Hattie asked as she came

into the kitchen and took baby Luther into her arms.

"Selma, Olive, Daisy, and Luther came this morning from Wells Township," I said as I pointed to each child.

"That's Olive, and that's Daisy," Selma said, correcting me and pointing to the twins.

"Welcome to Mama Hattie's house. It's a pleasure to meet you," Hattie said.

Mama Hattie's House, the perfect name for an orphanage.

"Looks like Luther could use a bath and something to eat. Are you girls hungry?" Hattie asked.

"Yes, ma'am," Selma said.

"Cora, show Selma how we gather eggs, and I'll make some sugar water for baby Luther."

"Yes, mama," I said. "Come with me, Selma."

Selma followed me outside and tugged on my apron.

"My mama died. My daddy died too."

"I know, Mrs. Frederick told me, I'm sorry. That's why you are here at Mama Hattie's house. I came here many years ago when my parents died too. Do you know how to read?"

"No," Selma said.

"I can teach you to read and write. Would you like that?"

"Yes, ma'am, I would."

We gathered eggs, enough to feed the new girls and the other ten children who called Mama Hattie's house home. We came back inside to find Hattie concerned. The look on her face told me, no need to speak of it and upset the girls further.

"Selma, does baby Luther ever cry?" Hattie asked.

"He did when he was born. But not much, nowadays."

"Poor child. I wish we had a wet nurse nearby, he's not going to make it," Hattie whispered. "His bottom was a bloody mess, and his breathing crackles. Hear it?"

I nodded. "Mrs. Frederick, the lady from Wells, said their daddy died from the consumption. I hope Baby Luther didn't get the consumption too."

"I'll keep him warm by the fire and feed him some goat's milk after we feed the others."

Hattie tied her apron into a sling that held baby Luther close to her chest. After breakfast and the morning chores, I started school with all the children. Hattie rocked baby Luther for hours, rubbing his back and humming lullabies until she nodded off herself.

Baby Luther died one week later. Hattie did her best to bring him to health, rocked him night and day, fed him everything she could think of.

"He was too sick when he got here last week," Hattie said.

"You did everything you could, Mama. I'm so sorry."

"So sad, I loved that boy the minute I laid eyes on him, but the good Lord called him home."

We buried Luther in our backyard cemetery. Luther was the fifth child to die and be buried at Mama Hattie's house.

The afternoon clamor left my head pounding, relentless motion, constant need of my attention. Where did Hattie go for her well of patience and grace? She had taken ill of late, and I tended to the children alone. Thank goodness Meriday and Lewis were coming Friday; Meriday to tend to Hattie and Lewis and their two, youngest boys to tend to some outside chores. Maybe Eli would make a surprise visit home too.

The older children helped with supper, chicken and dumplings for the children and broth for Hattie. The children got in bed, and the older children read stories to the young ones. I sat in the kitchen to catch up on my own reading. First, a letter from Eli.

My Dearest Cora,

I pray this letter finds you well. Construction on the Vanderbilt house, the Biltmore, will be completed in the coming months. I've learned much about the trades and life during the years of my absence. I have the skills necessary to adequately support a family and do it proudly. I have a store of money, and most importantly, I have proven myself a capable and worthy man. I pray that you find me worthy as well.

I received word that Mama has taken ill. My heart is heavy knowing she is not well. I will come home as soon as I am able.

You are forever my only love, my heart,

Elijah

Sweet Eli, he had always been worthy. My heart longed for him. I folded the letter and brought it to my nose, hoping to find a remnant of the author. I placed it in a wooden keepsake box filled with a decade of love and devotion from Eli.

Next, I read a letter from the State Legislature of North Carolina.

Dear Miss Cora Bateman of Westbrook,

We have reviewed your request for state funding for a Negro orphanage and regret to inform you that we are unable to honor your request at this time. If you elect to re-apply in the future, please do so under the auspices of a white, Christian man of upstanding character as required.

Regards,

Beauregard Fink

Under the auspices of a white, Christian man, that means as a colored woman, I'm not a person worthy of being taken seriously. There's only one white, Christian man who knows me, who owes me. But, I can't approach him alone, it wouldn't be proper, it wouldn't be safe. I'll save this for another day.

I checked on the boys' room. All was quiet, and the smell of boys lingered. Not a sound to be heard from the girls' room. Tending to Hattie came next. A bedside candle shined on the bloody rags. I placed a clean cloth in her hand for the coughing that will happen tonight. I brought the putrid bucket of liquid, bloody stool and soiled rags outside to be cleaned in the morning. I made a pallet next to Hattie, and sleep came as my head hit the pillow.

When morning came, I'd never been happier to see Lewis and Meriday. That's saying something as they are always a welcome sight, especially if they bring my nephews, Virgil and Otis. They reminded me of my brothers, loving each other one minute and fighting the next. Today, I needed them as I didn't have anything left to give.

"I'll tend to Hattie," Meriday said. "Let's see if she will get up today and take some fresh air on the porch."

"I'll teach the boys how to mend the fence," Lewis said.

"Thank you both, I'm barely standing."

I finished my morning chores and joined Hattie on the back porch. "It's good to see you up."

"The fresh air feels good," Hattie said as she coughed into a rag.

She looked at the red and then looked at me to see if I saw the blood. I looked away so she wouldn't know how I worried.

"Eli wrote to me and said he will be returning home soon."

"He has sure made something of himself by now," Hattie said.

"Yes, Mama. Eli is a good man." I leaned back and reached for my necklace.

"Tell me again about that necklace of yours," Hattie said.

"My mama gave it to me when I was a little girl. She said it had special powers, but she died before she could tell me about it."

"I have a similar necklace that my mama gave to me," Hattie said.

I leaned forward with excitement. "You never told me about that before. Where is it?"

"It's hidden in my room. Hidden from people who might want to steal it, even though it has no value to them."

"Can I see it?"

"In due time, Cora. In due time."

"Whoa, now," Eli said as his horse galloped into the yard, dragging an unwilling pack mule loaded down with Eli's belongings.

"Eli! You're home," Hattie said.

126

"Hello Mama," Eli said as he dismounted and handed the reins to Otis. Lewis untethered the mule and handed him off to Virgil.

"Boys, unload and water Uncle Eli's animals, you hear?" Lewis said.

"Yes, Papa."

Eli walked up the porch and nodded at me.

"Cora."

He reached down and kissed Mama on the head.

"It does my heart good to see you," Hattie said.

"Are you back in Westbrook for good?" I asked.

"I believe so, Lord willing."

"Now, that's a cause for celebration," Meriday said as she walked out of the house to greet Eli.

My head swirled with emotion, thrilled Eli was finally home, yet, worried that I would no longer be the object of Eli's affection. Silly. This homecoming was not about me. It was the proud son returning home to comfort his dying mother. Nothing was more important. Today was a good day. Eli and Lewis were back, Meriday and the boys too. Hattie was out of bed and getting some fresh air.

"Mama, can Otis and I go play down by the river?" Virgil said.

"Is all your work done?"

"Yes, ma'am."

"Yes. Be on time for supper," Meriday said.

Otis and Virgil gave Grandma Hattie a kiss, and they ran off to play. The remaining adults relaxed on the porch.

"Tell me about life in Asheville, Eli," Lewis said.

"Just a lot of people and a lot of work."

"I bet the mansion is beautiful," Hattie said.

"It's so big, we could house 1000 children there," Eli said.

"Wouldn't that be wonderful?" I said. "We could surely use more room for the children."

"And a much bigger kitchen," Hattie said.

"I think we should build a new orphanage here in Westbrook," Eli said.

"How on earth are we going to pay for that?" Hattie asked.

"I saved up some money over the years, and I know some people who can build things."

"I think that's a conversation for another day. We have more urgent things to discuss," I said.

"Mama, we are concerned that you are very sick and might leave this earth," Lewis said. "We need to know your wishes in case something happens to you."

"Well, that is depressing," Hattie said.

"Yes, very. But it is something we must discuss as a family," I said.

"I don't want to admit that my time here is coming to an end. But with the way this cough is going, I might be meeting Jesus sooner than I had hoped," Hattie said.

"Have you thought about what you would like to do with the house and the children?" Eli asked.

"I was hoping that you, my children, would carry on the work."

"I would like to see that happen. But, I can't take care of the children, the house, and the animals by myself," I said.

"Then we will have to find a way to make it work, Lord willing," Hattie said.

"Why don't we pray about it for a few days and see what the Lord reveals," Meriday said.

"I think that's a lovely idea. I'm getting tired now. Can one of you help me get back to bed?"

"I'll help you, Mama."

It not that I was eager to help Mama, but I wanted to ask about her necklace privately. I helped her out of the chair and steadied her as she walked to her bedroom.

"It looks like Meriday washed your bedding," I said as I helped Mama sit on her bed.

"She is very thoughtful," Hattie said before starting a coughing fit.

I handed her a clean rag and rubbed her back until she was able to breathe again.

"Let me help you get undressed."

"Thank you."

"Can you tell me more about your necklace now?"

"What do you want to know?"

"Well, can I see it?"

"Close the door and look to the hinges. There is a loose board just a few inches to the right. See it?"

I closed the door and felt for a loose board.

"Just a little further down," Hattie said.

I moved my hand down a little further and felt a board move.

"Now, just jiggle it a little bit, and the board should come out. My necklace is in a box hidden inside the hole."

I removed the board and reached for the box like I was reaching for a piece of gold. I handed the box to Hattie and waited to see what she would say.

"Thank you, Cora. I'm a little confused. I prayed that day for a daughter, and there you were. I prayed for a daughter, so I could pass this necklace to her. So, you came, just like I prayed, but you already had a talisman from your mama.

"I have this necklace. But, without the knowledge of what it means, it has no value other than a keepsake from my mother."

"I am the keeper of that knowledge."

"Can you tell me what it means, please?" Hattie began coughing again and gasping for air. I moved her feet up on the bed and lowered her head onto her pillow.

"Put some pillows behind me so I can sit up a little and breathe easier."

I propped some pillows behind her and held her hand in mine. Her hands bore the scars and calluses of a life well-lived.

"Cora?"

"Yes, Mama, I'm here."

"The necklace, you'll know when it's time. Go to the river, learn, and share your wisdom."

Her head turned away, and she took her last breath.

CHAPTER FIFTEEN

Amadahy

Aguaquiri
Harvest Moon, 1664

Love is love is love is love.
— Lin-Manuel Miranda

L eotie healed with time and was able to weave with Quatsey's help. We made baskets, mats for sleeping, and gifts for Gawonii. I was indebted to him for saving Leotie's life when she had the fever. We spent our days planting squash and corn, harvesting wild roots and flowers, and sharing days together. Quatsey and I met with the village medicine woman to learn her ways. Quatsey was eager to be with her like a hummingbird dancing with a flower, and I felt strangely jealous.

It came time for me to return to my village, check on my mother, and return Gawonii's canoe. Our brief trip to find Quatsey turned into many days and nights. I hoped that my transgression against Gawonii would be washed away like a leaf floating down the river.

"It's time to return to our village, Leotie."

"I don't want to go."

"I don't either, but like a full moon, we can only appear for a short while and return another day."

In my heart, I hoped Quatsey would beg us to stay or ask when we planned to return. But no. Quatsey helped us load our canoe and carry it to the river.

"Thank you for treating us like family and sharing your gift of weaving with us," I said.

"I am grateful for your visit," Quatsey said.

I noticed her necklace that connected us, but it remained a mystery.

"I hope our paths cross again soon."

"If it is to be, then it will be," Quatsey said.

I felt a chill, a cold wind pass between us.

Leotie and I found our seats in the canoe, and Quatsey pushed us into the river. I rowed home against the current and away from the woman I admired. Not a word passed between us as Leotie fixed her eyes on where we had been. We stopped midway home to eat and hoped for no uninvited guests. None came.

Mother stood in the fields when we returned. She thought us to be intruders and greeted us with a tool in her hand.

"Amadahy, Leotie! I thought you left for the spirit world."

"Hello, Mother. Forgive me for not sending word. We had a few problems with nature."

"A snake bit me," Leotie said as she showed her hand. "See the bite marks on my finger?"

"You could have met your sister in the spirit world with that."

"Mother," I said.

"I speak the truth," Mother said.

"Sometimes it's wise to leave the truth in the clouds."

I took in the sights of my home and village. Was this where I would spend the remainder of my days alone? Leotie would be with me, of course, and my mother in all her bitterness. I had my heart set on Quatsey, but she was with me for a short season. I had my daughter, she brought me purpose and returned my thoughts to gratitude.

"Leotie, help me return Gawonii's canoe. I hope he accepts our gifts in return for keeping it so long."

"Yes, Mama."

We walked to Gawonii's and were welcomed home by villagers along the way.

"I thought you met a tragic fate," said one.

"Thank you, Great Spirit for their safe return," said another.

Word of our return carried through the village like bees returning to their hive. We found Gawonii at home in prayer.

"Sorry to disturb you," I said.

"Amadahy, Leotie! You're alive. I was just praying for your spirits to safely transition to the next world."

"Thank you for the prayers. But, we are alive. Please forgive me for being gone so long. I hope I didn't add to your troubles."

"Any inconvenience is blotted out by your safe return."

"We brought you gifts," Leotie said as she handed him a woven box with a lid.

"I'm honored," Gawonii said as he accepted the box.

"See the brown and yellow cane? Quatsey taught us how to weave beautiful patterns. This has a mountain on the top," Leotie said.

"It is beautiful, thank you."

"We have a box for each of your medicines. Love and healing intentions are woven into each one," I said.

"This will benefit all our villagers."

On our walk home, I wondered what the root of my mother's bitterness was. Anger, sadness, grief -- typically came and stayed for a season. What brought her a lifetime of winter?

"Why is Grandmother angry?" Leotie asked.

"I don't know when or why her name changed to Unastisgi, the crazy one."

I found Mother squatting in the southwest corner of the house, clutching my grandmother's necklace, rocking back and forth. I couldn't make sense of her mumbling, and her eyes looked out to a distant land. I knelt down beside her and swept the hair from in front of her eyes. For the first time, I felt a wave of compassion for my bitter mother.

"It's alright, Mother. Amadahy is here."

Another first, I wrapped my arms around my mother like a protective bear. I was protecting and comforting the woman who withheld the same from me. My peculiar mother, cold and distant like freezing rain on the mountain tops.

"What's troubling you, Mother? What brings you fear and sadness?"

"They keep coming, evil spirits. They torment me when the sun comes up and when the sun goes down. Get away from me. You're evil too, you filthy, evil woman!"

I stood up, wiped my hands, and said, "I'm sorry you have to see this, Leotie."

"Why is she so mean?"

"I wish I knew."

Mother stayed in the corner throughout the night, talking to unseen spirits. She frightened me, but I knew it best to leave her alone when the evil spirits took over.

When the sun shone its first light, I could see Mother slumped over, asleep. I lit the hearth and prepared corn mush for breakfast. I cleaned and organized our neglected home, folded and stowed pelts in my new baskets, and stacked water vessels by the door, ready for a trip to the river.

"Are you ready to eat, Leotie?"

"Yes, Mama. What are we doing today?"

"We need to finish cleaning and check the food stores. Grandma needs to clean herself at the river; she didn't tend to anything while we were gone."

"Can we go to the river first?"

"We will go to the river after the sun moves to the west. Grandma needs to be warm."

Mother woke and ate breakfast with us. Her eyes looked past me, yet she was aware of our presence.

"How are you feeling today, Mother?"

"I'm awake and breathing. Don't concern yourself."

"Do you want to walk to the river with us later today?"

"All I want to do is sleep."

"Sleep if you must. Leotie and I have work to do."

Leotie and I left Mother alone and began our day.

"Let's harvest before the sun gets too hot."

"I've got an idea, and I need to find a branch. I'll be back," Leotie said as she turned and ran to the trees.

Her shiny black hair moved like the mane of a wild horse. Her graceful legs carried her, jumping over low brush. She returned carrying a branch as long as she was tall.

"Watch this," Leotie said, bursting with excitement.

She hung the handles of a new basket on each end and raised the branch over her head and rested it on her shoulders.

"See Mama, I can carry so much more this way."

"Look at you, wise as the village elders. Let's go to the fields and fill those baskets."

Halfway to the fields, I heard someone calling my name. "Amadahy! Amadahy! Come quickly."

I turned around to see Agayvlige Agatanai, a village elder walking toward us.

"What's wrong?"

"It's your mother. She is in the village center, wielding a knife, threatening to kill."

"She is not in her right mind. Leotie, find Gawonii and tell him Grandmother needs him. Thank you, Agatanai, for finding me. Let's go to her now."

"Run, Amadahy. I'll be there as fast as my old legs can carry me."

I ran to the village center to find my mother naked, screaming at people who weren't there.

"You, with long hair, I see you. You came here to hurt me again. But, I'm ready for you this time."

Villagers peered from behind trees and homes. Some appeared frightened while others pointed and sneered at the old fool. Four young men quietly gathered behind Mother, one man signaled directions with his hands. They spread out into a semicircle behind her.

"Mother, look at me," I said, hoping to keep her eyes looking forward.

In one swift and coordinated movement, the men took her knife and cradled her to the ground. Relieved no one was injured, I once again knelt by my mother to comfort her. Her vacant eyes told me the evil spirits controlled her still. Villagers came out to stare, and I felt the heat rising up my face.

"Let go of me, you evil woman," Mother hissed through clenched teeth.

She looked like a wild cat, injured and frightened.

"It's me, Amadahy. You're safe now, no one can hurt you."

"Get away from me."

Mother pushed me, jumped up, defying her years, and ran out of the village. More village chatter shamed me. She was my mother, my responsibility. I sat on the ground, knowing it was of no use to chase her. I held my head down and covering my eyes, hiding my tears. I felt a touch on my shoulder.

"Stand up, Amadahy. Come, walk with me," Agayvlige Agatanai said.

I picked my grandmother's necklace off the ground and did as the village elder told me. I followed Agatanai until we came upon a circle of six elders. The women, all tribal grandmothers, were of my mother's generation. I sat and feared a scolding, so I fixed my eyes to the ground and rubbed my fingers over my grandmother's necklace. Agatanai joined us.

"All life is sacred, Amadahy, as is your mother's life. She is not well, and evil spirits are speaking through her," Agatanai said.

The women around the circle nodded in agreement.

"My mother is cold and distant, like snow on top of the mountain range. Yet, I have never seen her act this way in front of villagers before. You have known my mother her whole life on earth. What happened to her? I do not understand."

"Yes, we have known your mother all of our days. When we were innocent, she was curious, much like your daughter, Ahyoka. Her troubles began when she married your father, Chuquilatague."

"Tell me about my father. I never knew him, and my mother never speaks of him."

"Chuquilatague, meaning double-headed, appeared to be a good husband by day and cruel by night. Like an injured wolf bites the giving hand, your father hurt your mother because he had been hurt. In turn, your mother is cruel to you," Agatanai said.

"Even so, I would never hurt my child," I said.

"You are strong and have broken the cycle of cruelty."

"Why, then, is my heart still broken? How has my mother transformed from hurt to cruel, to out of her mind?"

"So many questions, so few answers. You have suffered great loss, sorrow is expected."

"What happened to my father? Did my mother kill him?"

"No, but he nearly killed her. Before your life in her womb was known, your father beat her until she was near death. Knowing he would be banished from the tribe for his actions, your father vanished with their two sons, leaving your mother for dead," Agatanai said.

The anguish came over me like hail in a summer storm. It didn't make sense, and the pain was unbearable. My head felt light, my breath sparse. Brothers? I had two brothers? No one honored them by speaking their names.

"Where did they go? Are they alive?"

"Only they and the wind know."

"This is too much for me to breathe in."

"It is a heavy weight to bear," Agatanai said. "But it does help us understand why your mother's mind is no longer grounded on the earth."

Pointing to my grandmother's necklace, Agatanai asked, "Do you know the power you hold in your hand?"

"It is my grandmother's necklace. I don't think it has any special power."

"It does, Amadahy. Its power will be revealed when you're ready."

Gawonii approached the circle and waited to be acknowledged. Even a revered spiritual leader knew not to impose upon the tribal grandmothers without permission.

"Yes, Gawonii?" Agatanai nodded.

"Forgive my interruption, esteemed elders. I wanted to ease Amadahy's mind and let her know that we found her mother. I gave her some medicine, and she is resting at home. Leotie returned to the field to finish her harvest."

"Thank you, Gawonii. I am relieved to hear it," I said.

Gawonii nodded in respect to the elders, turned around, and walked toward the village.

"Thank you for telling my family's secret. As difficult as it is to hear, it does shed light on my past and my mother's pain."

"We are family in this village, connected like streams to the river. When you have sorrow, we mourn with you. When you have a reason for joy, we all celebrate," Agatanai said.

"There is something else weighing on my heart. I could use your wise counsel if you find me worthy."

"Of course."

"I've found love in a village to the south. But, I'm not certain that feeling is returned. How do I know?"

"Love is a mystery, Amadahy. It surrounds us like the air we breathe, yet we don't take notice unless we breathe it in deeply." Agatanai paused and looked to Immokalee, inviting her to speak.

"Is this man willing to leave his village and join ours?"

"That's my concern, Immokalee. The person I love is a woman."

"Love knows no gender. It is a connection of spirits, not genitalia." The elders nodded in agreement.

"I'm relieved you accept my love for Quatsey. I yearn to feel her love in return. Tell me, in the tradition of our foremothers, would she join our village, or would I move to her village to the south?"

"Either way is acceptable. Consider your mother and Leotie, they must go with you. Is this Quatsey you speak of living with a large family?" Immokalee asked.

"She is alone."

"That is unusual for a person to have no family living in the same home. Given your mother's torment, it would be better for you to remain here."

"It may just be a dream that I will ever have to make that decision."

"Love is here Amadahy, just breathe it in," Immokalee said.

The elders stood and looked to Agatanai, I followed their lead. Agatanai raised her arms to the sky and prayed,

"Grandmothers in the spirit world, remind us that love is what connects us.

Love connects us to all that is living and grounds us to the earth that sustains us.

Foremothers, guide our sister, Amadahy, in grieving her past.

Foremothers, guide our sister, Amadahy, in seeking new love.

Guide her in finding purpose and joy in this world, leaving a legacy for her daughter, Leotie, and for Leotie's daughters to come."

Agatanai lowered her arms, turned, and walked toward the village. We all followed in silence, except for my involuntary gasp when I noticed my grandmother's necklace glowing in my hand.

I returned home to find Leotie filling the larder with the morning harvest. She worked with confidence and peace, still possessing child-like innocence amid life-altering trauma. Was she prepared for womanhood, like a bird who is prepared to fly from the nest? Not yet. I needed her.

"Hi, Mama. Are you okay?"

"Yes. I spent time with the tribal elders; the grandmothers' guidance was enlightening."

"Look, I filled this whole basket with berries. I feel Ahyoka's spirit when I walk along, looking to the earth for food to sustain us."

"That's a beautiful connection. Let's go inside and enjoy the berries. Ahyoka can join us too."

I put my arm around Leotie's shoulder and gave her a squeeze, communicating my love, protection, and pride.

"Mama, that necklace is bright." Leotie took the necklace

into her hand. "Ow! It's hot!" she said as it dropped it on the ground.

"Understanding will come when we are ready."

I bent down to pick up the necklace and tied it around my neck. I put my arm around Leotie's shoulders again, and we walked inside to share the bounty of her harvest. I saw my mother resting on her mat, a woman tended to her.

"Hello?"

My heart stopped; did my eyes deceive me as they adjusted to the darkness? Could it be? A tall, muscular woman turned toward me as she grew to a standing position. Her necklace glowed on her chest and illuminated her face. It was Quatsey, we moved toward each and into a lover's embrace. Our necklaces touched, and I heard a crackling sound like lighting piercing the sky.

CHAPTER SIXTEEN

At the River

We all belong to an ancient identity. Stories
are the rivers that take us there.
— Frank Delaney

T he riverbank appeared much the same, dense foliage, the
scent of damp earth. Nature's song played in the back-
ground; birds sang, crickets chirped, water cascaded
over stones and fallen tree limbs. If you listened carefully, you
could hear the breeze play harmony on the river cane. This was
a magical space, hidden in plain sight. Women spent time here
during their own centuries to gather food, bathe, celebrate, or
connect with nature. Now they returned to the river, not by
conscious choice, but compelled by the power of their maternal talismans.

Janene came first, healthy and vibrant. She appeared at the
riverbank, eyes and mouth opened in disbelief. Arms stretched
to the sky; hands reached for the stars. Legs marched without
struggle, and feet jump on command. She flipped her hair back
and laughed at the sky.

"Jesus Christ! I must be dead!"

Cora appeared on the riverbank. "Jesus? Did you see Jesus?"

"No. But I can walk and talk again. So, I must be dead. Who are
you?"

"My name is Cora. Pleased to make your acquaintance," she said with a nod, looking down to avoid eye contact with Janene. "It's mighty strange, ma'am, happening into you this way."

Cora looked at Janene, puzzled. Yet, curiosity won over manners.

"Pardon me. But, are those your husband's britches? He must be a slight man, seeing as they are wrapped around your legs so tightly."

"Hi, Cora. I'm Janene." She pinched her jeans, pulled the fabric, and released it to snap against her thigh. "No. Just my stretch jeans. Are you dead too?"

"I'm quite alive, thank you."

"Are you part of a Civil War reenactment? That's the most authentic period costume I've ever seen."

"Goodness, no. Who would want to reenact such a nightmare? I thanked the good Lord when the war finally ended."

Amadahy stepped out from behind the tree, where she had watched the conversation between Janene and Cora unfold. Amadahy stood silently with her chin high and arms at her side. Her confidence heightened her beauty. Janene and Cora turned to Amadahy, waiting for her to speak.

"I am Amadahy of the Wolf Clan."

Although Amadahy spoke in the language of her ancestors, the three women understood each other.

After a prolonged silence, Janene said, "I've seen you before, Amadahy. There's a painting of you hanging in the office of Westbrook High School. It's stunning."

Amadahy contemplated Janene's words, unable to make sense of them. The three women stood through the awkward silence. "I'm glad it brings you happiness. Yet, I find this all very strange."

"Strange indeed," Cora said. "Maybe our meeting is what Mama Hattie told me about. Do you have a necklace like this?"

Cora removed her necklace and extended it to Amadahy and Janene.

"Yes," they replied. "My grandmother told me I'd know what

to do with it when the time was right. She said something about the power of sisterhood," Janene said.

"Sisterhood? I don't have any sisters," Cora said.

"Neither do I," Amadahy said. "I have no sisters in my village by birth. But, you could be my sisters through the power of this talisman."

"Where is your village?" Cora asked. "I live on Main Street in Westbrook."

"I live in the village of Aguaquiri. It's a stone's throw from here, just west of the river."

"Aguaquiri? That's where the Eastern Band of the Cherokee lived before European settlers pushed the indigenous people out. Later the town was known as Westbrook." Janene was thankful for the years she studied regional history. "I live in Westbrook too."

"We are sisters by the river," Cora said.

The sisters discovered the secret of the talisman; it brought them together at the river, sans the dimension of time. Women, regardless of century or culture, gathered to support and encourage one another.

"We are all connected," Amadahy said as she scanned the riverbank for a suitable place to sit.

She took a few steps, bent down, and tossed some rocks aside. Janene and Cora watched Amadahy move with purpose. She untied a cane mat from her back and unrolled it on the ground.

"Please, join me," Amadahy said with her arms opened toward the mat.

Janene and Cora approached. "It's beautiful," Cora said. "I've never seen anything like it."

"Thank you. Quatsey, the basket weaver, taught me. Please, sit," Amadahy said as she sat cross-legged on the mat, facing the river. The other two joined her. Cora swept her dress under her legs to her left; Janene sat cross-legged too, giddy that her body was working again.

"Janene, may I ask why you think yourself to be dead?" Cora

said.

Janene leaned forward with her elbows perched on her knees. "I have to be. I had a fatal disease, couldn't walk or talk. I was paralyzed. Now, look at me!"

"We are together, though not bound by the laws of space and time. We will return when the time is right," Amadahy said.

"I don't want to return to my broken body and my miserable life. No thanks. I'm done suffering."

"You have suffered dearly, for what purpose?" Amadahy asked.

"I have no idea why I've suffered so horribly."

"Death is a part of life. One cannot avoid it," Amadahy said.

"Death, sure. We all are going to die. But why the suffering? Why me?"

"We all suffer pain and loss. My daughter died from a fever," Amadahy said.

"When I was a little girl, my parents and brothers were murdered," Cora said. Tears welled, she buried her grief six feet deep, like a corpse, hoping it never surfaced. She feared the floodgates opening, not knowing if she could return from the depths of her sorrow. Cora stuffed her feelings again like she did that morning Hattie and the boys discovered her identity. Survival surpassed grief.

"My family died in a car accident when I was young. My grandma raised me," Janene said. "Aren't we a sorry mess?"

Amadahy reached into her medicine pouch and pulled out a small leather bag. She poured her prayer stones onto the mat and arranged them into a prayer circle, instinctively knowing true north. Amadahy leaned her head back, paying respects to her ancestors, and silently asked the Great Spirit for guidance.

Cora clasped her hands in her lap and prayed. "Oh, sweet Jesus, you say in your good book that when two or more are gathered in your name, you will be in the midst of us. Thank ye for thy presence. Amen." Cora's head remained bowed, and Amadahy continued to gaze skyward. Janene noticed three women walking toward them from behind the trees.

"I don't think we're alone."

Cora and Amadahy looked at the three approaching women who wore flowing linen robes, dyed in nature's hues.

The leading woman, a crone with freckled, white skin, said, "Cora, Amadahy, and Janene, welcome to the sisterhood. We are here to hold a safe and supportive space for you."

"Are you in charge? I'd like to know if I am dead and what we are doing here."

"No one is in charge. We are a collective of women. I'm Ruth, and these are your sisters."

Ruth spread her arms open to the hundreds of women who now joined in a circle around the fledgling timeless sisters. Women of the world, from every tribe and nation, past and present, wearing every color under the sun, had one thing in common. They believed in the power of sisterhood.

"This is mind-blowing. I've never felt anything so powerful," Janene said.

"The Great Spirit has lifted me from the earth and placed me in the clouds."

"I feel Mama Ada and Mama Hattie here with me."

"You are experiencing the collective spirit of sisterhood. The veil has been lifted, and you know that you are not alone."

Women formed a large circle and stood in support around Janene, Cora, and Amadahy. Tiny spheres of light floated among them like stardust, and clouds covered the ground. A chorus of drums sent healing vibrations through the circle. Soothing chants helped the women clear their minds of worry. The atmosphere left no doubt that the women had entered a new dimension.

"We are holding a sacred space of healing for you. There is no judgment, only loving support. You are free to share your story or not. We are here for you," Ruth said.

"I'd like to start," Cora said.

Ruth nodded, encouraging Cora to continue.

"I have a secret that brings me shame. Deep down, I feel broken."

Cora straightened her back, summoning the courage to continue.

"I am barely considered a person by most standards, I've precious little control over my life."

"What do you want to control?" Amadahy asked?

"My place in society, how others treat me as less than, less than human because my skin is black."

"Race is a social construct, designed by those in power, to oppress and divide. It serves no other purpose," Janene said.

"Whoever started it, it's sure working to keep colored folks and women in our place. There's nothing we can do about it."

"Don't let that define who you are. My Grandma Betty said the only thing that we can control is how we respond. Women who overcome injustice and being treated so poorly are typically the strongest people. How did you survive after your family was murdered?"

"Elijah and Lewis, Mama Hattie's sons, found me under a tree after I ran away from the Yarbrough plantation. They took me home, and Hattie raised me as her own. She took care of lots of Negro orphans along the way." Cora wiped her nose with her apron. "The consumption just took Hattie, haven't had the chance to bury her yet."

"I'm sorry about Hattie. I know it's hard," Janene said.

"I'm so grateful, I would have been beaten to near-death if someone else had found me under that tree and returned me to Master Yarbrough. They'd made me a sure example. Fortunately, Eli and Lewis found me first." Cora stopped and grinned. "Eli has been sweet on me since I became grown. He even asked me to marry him. He's a good man, I know my daddy would have approved."

"Did you marry Eli?" Amadahy asked.

"No, it wouldn't be proper. Eli deserves someone clean and pure, a virgin. The man who attacked me said he made me a whore. I'm not good enough, I don't deserve the likes of him."

"That's nonsense, Cora. You were raped, that doesn't make you a whore. It's not your fault," Janene said.

"I can't make it right. Eli would never accept me if he knew the truth."

"You say he is a good man?" Amadahy asked.

"Yes, an honorable man."

"Then, maybe you are assuming incorrectly what he will do," Amadahy said.

"If Eli loves you, what happened to you in the past won't matter to him," Janene said. "What does Jesus say about you?"

"The book of Romans says that God commendeth his love toward us, in that, while we were yet sinners, Christ died for us. Then it says neither height, nor depth, nor any other creature, shall be able to separate us from the love of God, which is in Christ Jesus our Lord."

"If you're good enough for Jesus, then you are good enough for Eli," Janene said.

"I don't know your Jesus. But I do know that, through our ancestors, the Great Spirit says all life is sacred and worthy of respect," Amadahy said.

"I know all this in my head, but I never believed it in my heart. No matter where I go, I'm reminded that I am a colored woman. I'm a low rung on society's ladder, just not good enough."

"What you believe about yourself is true until you change the story in your mind," Amadahy said.

"You are right on, Amadahy. You need to change the story you tell yourself. You are powerful, worthy of love and happiness, worthy of Eli's love."

Cora took in what her timeless sisters said. The words traveled from her head and bounced off the walled fortress of Cora's heart.

"I hear what you are saying, it makes sense. Why can't I believe it?"

"What do you gain by closing off your heart?" Amadahy asked.

"I've no idea."

"You're afraid," Janene said.

"Well, of course, I'm afraid. I've lived my whole life in fear. You know how colored people can disappear, and nobody pays any mind."

"I can't imagine how traumatic that must be. I'm talking about the fear you have of loving someone so deeply that you fear you couldn't survive if you lost them. It's safer to not marry Eli. You may be sad and lonely, but your heart can't be broken if you're alone," Janene said.

"I've never thought about it like that before."

"Think about it, Cora. You are a special woman, caring and loving, worthy of love. Take a risk with your heart and give Eli a chance."

Cora smiled. Butterflies of young love danced on her heart. Thoughts of growing old with Eli sparked hope.

Amadahy stood up and walked toward the riverbank. The women in the circle parted, giving her way. Squatting, she felt the current with her hand. Amadahy stood and removed her loincloth and leather bodice and placed them on a rock for safekeeping. Unashamed of her body, displaying childbearing's toll and scars of a labored life, Amadahy stepped into the river, as though she returned to a place of comfort. Turning north, she submerged.

"Our sister from another mister is taking a bath," Janene said as she nudged Cora.

Cora saw Amadahy emerge from the river. "Apparently so."

Janene and Cora watched Amadahy disappear and reappear six more times. Amadahy walked out of the river and sat on a rock. She found a spot where the sun peeked through the canopy, hugged her knees, and stared at the river.

Janene walked toward Amadahy and sat down next to her. "What's on your mind?"

"Cleansing in the river reminds me that everything is sacred and connected. When I feel troubled, out of balance, the river washes me clean of unhealthy thoughts I carry. It's a rebirth of sorts. The burdens are not mine to carry. They weigh my spirit down until I suffocate, like a fire deprived of wind. In this way, I cannot be present nor experience gratitude."

"I understand that feeling. It's like a dark cloud, pressing down. I can't get out from under it, at times I can feel my heart racing. I perseverate on my own drama, chasing thoughts, on and on. I can't see any way out," Janene said. "I can't make any sense of it. It's a miserable way to live."

Amadahy dressed and returned to the cane mat, Janene followed. "I feel that way too, sometimes," Cora said

"Tell us your story, Amadahy," Cora said.

Amadahy looked at Cora and Janene, checking her sixth sense. Her survival depended on her ability to discern who and what imposed danger. She counted her girls, Gawonii, with a healthy fear, and most recently Quatsey as the only people in her life with whom she felt safe. Others cared only for themselves and used any signs of vulnerability against her. Could she trust her timeless sisters? Amadahy sensed they could be trusted.

"The people in my village work together for physical survival, we work the harvest together and share the bounty, men make sure everyone benefits from the hunt. But that's the extent of care. I just want to be accepted and valued for who I am, even as I'm often the topic of discussion at the grinding stones. They call me u-tso-s-da-ne-hi, the awkward one. I've never fit in."

"You feel alone," Cora said.

"I dance to my own drumbeat and fly like the lone eagle. That's my life, yet, I'm tired of walking alone. My husband left me, and one of my daughters died. My daughter, Leoti, and I mourned. I thought the sun would never rise again."

"You have to mourn," Janene said.

"Then, I met Quatsey in the lavender meadow by the river. Like a new sun rising, she brings light to my life. I feel joy returning in the next season. I can't let fear keep me in darkness."

"What do you fear?" Cora asked.

"A broken heart, being abandoned like the wolf leaves a deformed pup. But, no more. I'm walking through the fear like the sun's rays poking through dark clouds."

"Praise be, Amadahy," Cora said.

Cora and Amadahy's smiles emanated joy and peace. Cora held her head high and shoulders square. The lines of distrust etched in Amadahy's forehead softened. Janene observed them with a hint of jealousy.

"I'm happy for you both," Janene said. "I'm going to miss my family, but thankful that I'm free from my broken body. It was unbearable."

"I'm hoping to return to Westbrook and tell Eli yes, for better or worse. What if," Cora hesitated. "What if we all return to our lives as they were?"

"Oh god, I hope not," Janene said.

"You should prepare for that to happen," Amadahy said. "I can't imagine being trapped inside a body that has betrayed me."

"It's like being imprisoned for a crime you didn't commit," Janene said.

"I can't imagine what you've experienced either," Cora said. "I do know what it is like to be owned, to not know freedom. And, I know what it is to live with my mind behind bars, even as my body walks free."

Janene contemplated her body without the ravages of ALS. She inhaled the fragrant air, taking note of the ease of breathing with a fully-functional diaphragm. As much as she will miss her family, staying put in her healthy body appealed to her more than returning to her life, imprisoned in body and mind.

"My life wasn't supposed to turn out like this," Janene said to no one in particular, staring at the river's current. She took note that her life passed as swiftly as the leaf she watched float down the river.

"What were you expecting?" Amadahy asked.

"I expected to live a long and healthy life, retire, and play with my grandchildren. That's not going to happen."

"The Bible says in the book of James that we don't know what tomorrow brings. For what is your life? I can't remember the rest," Cora grimaced and tapped her temple with her index finger. "I remember now. It's like a vapor that appears for a little while and vanishes. That's it."

"The ancestors say that life is like the wind, blowing to and fro. Who can predict where it will go?" Amadahy said.

"I think unmet expectations are a sure cause of disappointment. It's no wonder you feel the way you do," Cora said.

"Let your expectations be like seeds in the wind, content to grow wherever they land," Amadahy said.

"Hanging on to what I thought should have happened has not served me well. It has brought me nothing but sorrow. But, I hang on, thinking that I must protest the injustice. Perhaps it's time for me to accept the hand that life dealt me," Janene said, amused that she could make sense of it all. Finally, some clarity.

"It's time to let go of fear and expectations. I wonder if I can practice peace and gratitude, regardless of circumstances?" Janene said.

"Yes," Cora said. "I am grateful that we've had this time together."

"I hope our paths cross again," Amadahy said as she reached for the talisman around her neck. "I will carry you both close to my heart. And, Thank you, Ruth and all my sisters for being here."

"It is our pleasure and honor to be here with you. We all face struggles in life, no one is exempt. So, remember this day and know that the collective sisterhood is with you in spirit. You are not alone." Ruth bowed her head, and the gathering of women returned to the trees.

The timeless sisters stood, ready to return to their lives. Amadahy rolled her mat and disappeared into the woods, silently as she appeared. Cora and Janene embraced.

"My best to you, Janene. May God bless you on your journey."

"Thank you, Cora. I wish you and Eli years of happiness."

She watched Cora whisk away with her long skirt bouncing behind her. Janene stood at the riverbank, hesitant to return to her life. She marveled at her healthy body and ran her fingers through her hair one last time.

CHAPTER SEVENTEEN

Janene

Westbrook, North Carolina
2015

The purpose of life is not to be happy. It is to be useful,
to be honorable, to be compassionate, to have it make
some difference that you have lived and lived well.
— Ralph Waldo Emerson

I awoke on the beach, stuck in my chair. My talisman no longer glowed. "That was a weird dream."

"Dream? It's more like a nightmare. Grandma Betty is gone."

"I know, Hannah. But, I had this dream. There were two women. And I was healthy and strong."

"That's great, Mom. But, now we're back to reality. Dad is on his way to pick us up and take us back to Grandma's house. We've got to figure out how to get her affairs in order."

My present reality felt like an ill-fitting dress after the serene experience at the river. The time came to refocus and reframe. I wanted to put my new life-approach to the test.

"You're right, honey. It's going to be tough. But, we will get through it together."

Hannah stopped packing our beach supplies, tilted her head,

and looked at me. She tilted her head to the other side, looking like a confused Labrador puppy, and resumed packing. Tom and Daniel walked up, Tom bent down and kissed my forehead, Daniel hugged his sister.

"I'm sorry, Janene. I know how much you loved Grandma Betty," Tom said.

"I'm grateful for the years we had together. She had a life well-lived."

"Let's get you back in your chair and loaded into the van," Tom said.

Hannah and Daniel packed our beach day supplies in the van, and we drove to Grandma's house. By the time we arrived, the paramedics had zipped Grandma into a body bag and rolled the gurney into the ambulance. A paramedic shut the ambulance bay doors and walked toward us.

"Good morning, sir, ma'am. My name is Wilson. I'm sorry for your loss. Miss Betty was a legend in these parts." Wilson, a handsome young man, took off his hat and lowered his head. "We're really going to miss her around here."

"Thank you, Wilson. She was quite a lady," Tom said.

"I best be going. We are taking her body to the county hospital morgue for a routine autopsy. Someone from the county will give you a call when they're done." Wilson nodded in respect, put on his hat, and walked back to the ambulance.

I turned my power chair facing the house and drank in a lifetime of memories, Grandma, cousins, this house, the pain of loss, the joy of family, hallmarks of abundant life. My heart overflowed with gratitude, and a tear snuck down my cheek. Tom walked up behind me and placed his hand on my shoulder. My first thought was that Tom must be repulsed by the feel of my wasted shoulders, bones sticking out. Then, recognizing that negative thinking isn't helpful, I dismissed that thought and opened my heart to Tom's affection. My new way of being took practice. Tom, the kids, and I sat in the backyard, reminiscing, and discussing how to manage Grandma's estate.

"I found Grandma's will in her desk. She wants to be cremated and have her ashes spread here in the ocean. That we can do. Look," Tom said as he put some papers in the middle of the table. "Betty prearranged and prepaid for everything. She even picked out her urn."

"Of course she did," I said. "What does she want us to do with the house?"

"Her will says it belongs to us, and we can decide if we want to keep it or sell."

"I say we keep it," Daniel said.

"Me too," Hannah said. "I'd like to have some of her jewelry if that's okay."

"Sure, you can. It's great news that Grandma has everything in order. Maybe we can enjoy the rest of our vacation," Tom said.

"That's what Grandma would have wanted. Let's clean out the kitchen and close up the house. I mean you all do that. I can't get in the house, so I'll stay out here and take a nap."

We spent the rest of the week on the coast and spread half of Grandma's ashes in the ocean. I saved half of her to take home with me in her new urn.

I was relieved to be home and back into my hospital bed. My stiff joints and tender skin needed more support than a hotel bed provided. I thought the trip to the coast was my last. I didn't feel sad about it, rather thankful to have gone, and more thankful that my failing body wouldn't have to endure the difficulties of travel.

Daniel knocked on my bedroom door. "You awake, Mom?"

"Yes, come in," I mumbled in my tired voice.

Daniel walked in, sat on the side of my bed, and caressed my hand. It reminded me of when he was a baby and would rub my finger for comfort.

"I'm glad you're here with us."

We sat together, speaking a lifetime of love without words. I grew tired using my remaining torso muscles to breathe like a toddler recovering from a tantrum. I knew my days were short. I didn't want to die, I didn't want my family to see me struggle, I didn't want to suffer. So many wants over which I had no con-

154

trol. I focused my thoughts on gratitude, being present.

I looked at my computer to wake it up and gazed at each letter, determined to be heard.

"Daniel, please get your dad and sister. I've got something I want to tell you all."

"Dad. Hannah. Mom wants you in the living room!" Daniel said.

I kept my eyes on the screen as the family gathered in the living room. They knew to wait until I was done typing what I wanted to say. I locked in on the icon that tells my computer to speak and let out an inaudible sigh.

"You know my time is limited, and it's time we talk about it. I don't want a tracheotomy for life support, and I'm suffering more than I care to admit."

Hannah tried to interject, "But, Mom."

Without a pause button, I continued talking over her. Hannah slumped back into the couch, knowing she would have to wait her turn.

"I want to have a party here at the house to celebrate my life before I die. What do you think?"

Tom spoke up, breaking the awkward silence.

"What kind of party?"

"A celebration of life, before I die instead of after. I'm not having a wake. So, if people want to see my face, they need to come and see me before I go."

"That seems weird," Tom said.

"How do you want to celebrate?" Hannah asked.

"Just a BBQ in the backyard. What do you think, Daniel?"

Daniel looked up from his phone, "Whatever you want."

"Can't we just have friends over, not make a big deal out of it?" Tom asked.

"I'm down for a party. But, I don't want you to die, Mom," Hannah said on the verge of tears.

"I'm not in the mood to celebrate. I don't even want to talk about losing you, Janene."

I returned to my computer to type my response. "I know it's

hard for all of us. We don't handle death well. We're taught not to talk about it. But, the reality is, I'm dying. There's no way to stop this beast. I'm in constant pain, I can't scratch my nose or cough on my own. I'm sad that I'm going to miss your weddings, and that I will never see my grandchildren. But, soon I won't be able to breathe."

"Have you thought about going on a ventilator?" Tom asked.

"I've thought about it every day since my diagnosis. It's a huge step. I'd require 24/7 care. And the extra equipment and expense, insurance doesn't begin to cover it."

"You being here is more important than all of that," Hannah said.

"I respect your feelings about that, Hannah. I do. I'd given anything to have my mom with me. It just wasn't meant to be," I said.

"Well, that's messed up. I look at my old friends who are so deep in their addictions, they don't care if they live or die. And, here you are, fighting for your life. You're dying, it's not fair," Daniel said.

I waited for Daniel's dramatic exit, his way of avoiding an awkward conversation. But, he remained.

"It must be hard for you to see your friends struggle," Tom said.

"Yeah, it sucks."

Hannah put her arm around Daniel's shoulders, and the four of us sat in silence.

One month later, Hannah got me ready for my party. "Red dress?" she asked as she slid hangers to the right. She stopped and looked to see if I blinked yes.

"No? Something more comfortable?"

I blinked, "Yes."

No buttons, no zippers, only stretchy fabric, and elastic waistbands for me.

"Here, these crazy pants and a purple shirt."

I blinked, "Yes."

"Perfect, I'll get your silver earrings, too."

Hannah finished dressing me. I relaxed into the process, dismissing the frustration of not having control. Hannah's touch was extraordinarily gentle, conveying love and compassion. She rolled me into the kitchen and poured formula into my feeding tube.

"Watching everyone eat Daddy's brisket won't be as painful on a full stomach," I said. "Pour some of the good wine in there, while you're at it."

"Nothing but the best zin in a box for you, Mama."

"You look beautiful," Tom said as he came into the kitchen and kissed me on the forehead. "Let's head out into the backyard. Folks are here already."

Tom rolled me outside to the cheers of 100 of my closest friends. Love flooded my heart as I recognized the familiar faces of former students, along with neighbors and coworkers. Lisa emerged from the crowd with soft, brown curls where her headscarf had been. She walked toward me unencumbered, shoulders back, clear-eyed. She brought her cheek close to mine.

"No detectable cancer."

Lisa, my miracle friend, held my hand.

Justin, wearing his Army dress uniform, stood with a microphone.

"Mrs. Branch, we are all here to honor you. I want to take a minute to tell you how important you are to me. You were my teacher and you taught me so much more than history. When I felt like the world was crashing in around me, you taught me that hard times don't last forever. You told me to persevere, brighter days will come. That lesson served me well in the desert of Afghanistan. The nights were long, the enemy was close. I heard your voice telling me to hang in there, hard times don't last forever. Your words got me through some tough nights. Thank you."

Justin handed the microphone to Kristen and walked towards me. As I leaned in for a hug, I could smell the wool of his jacket. Kristen held the microphone and pushed her long brown hair behind her ears. Her eyes looked up, and she fanned her fingers in front of her face. She exhaled and said,

"Mrs. B., I'm having a hard time coming up with the words to tell you what you mean to me."

Kristen looked down and shifted her weight back and forth, knees bending. She looked back at me and said, "You believed in me when I didn't believe in myself. Thank you for loving me when I felt unlovable."

The crowd clapped, and a man I didn't recognize reached for the microphone and looked up at me through thick black glasses and frizzy brown curls.

"Hi. My name is Howard, Howard Taylor, from the class of '94. You probably don't remember me; I barely spoke at school."

Oh, Howie. Of course, I remember you.

"Anyway, I came here today to say thank you. Thank you for igniting my passion for history. Because of your passion, I've spent the last 20 years studying the correspondence of Union and Confederate soldiers. I now teach in the Department of Civil War Studies at Duke."

A handsome young man took the microphone to address the crowd.

"My name is Waya Aholokee from the Qualla Boundary. You gave me a precious gift, Mrs. Branch. Throughout my schooling, I felt accepted but less than my white classmates. But you, you celebrated my heritage. In a way, you gave me permission to be proud to be who I am and thankful for my Cherokee roots. So, I thank you."

I could scarcely breathe. I'd never considered the depth and breadth of lives touched during my years of teaching. I treasured every face, cherished every story. I made a difference.

CHAPTER EIGHTEEN

Cora

Westbrook, North Carolina
1895

The course of true love never did run smooth.
— William Shakespeare

I awoke from my dream, seated next to Hattie's body. "Sweet Jesus, Hattie's gone home to you. I'm going to miss her. Please welcome her to your eternal home, give me the strength to inter Hattie, and carry on without her."

How strange it is that I fell asleep right after Hattie passed. Did I meet my timeless sisters in a dream, or was it real? Sure as I'm sitting here, I'd swear it was real. I stayed composed so I could tell the others about Hattie's passing.

I straightened Hattie's dress and placed her hands on her lap. I returned Hattie's necklace to its hiding place. Then, I gathered the soiled rags and attempted to hide them from view. They weren't fit to be seen. I walked out of Hattie's room and paused in the doorway. I felt faint as old feelings of grief and abandonment kicked me in the stomach. I turned to Hattie and whispered, "Thank you."

I walked to the back porch to share the news of Hattie's passing.

"She's gone."

"No," Meriday said sobbing as she embraced Lewis. Eli walked to me with his arms held wide. I fell into his safe refuge, welcoming his strong arms and inhaled the lingering scent of dust and sweat from his journey home.

Three days later, we buried Hattie next to the children who passed. Eli said a few words to the people who gathered to pay their respects.

"Dear Lord Jesus, today, we commit Mama Hattie's body to the ground and her spirit to abide with you for all eternity. We will miss her presence here but rejoice in knowing she is with you in Heaven. Amen."

Eli extended his hand to Hattie as he walked past her pine coffin box. I wiped my tears and ran my hands down the side of my dress. My rough skin caught on the fabric. I rubbed my hands together, taking note of how dry they were. Lard, I said to myself. A good rubbing of lard would take care of that.

"You did Mama proud," I said to Eli as he approached.

"I hope so."

I hugged Eli and whispered in his ear, "The children and I are going to need you now more than ever."

"Need me? When have you ever needed me?"

"I've always needed you," I said, staring straight into his eyes. Ashamed of my forwardness, I stepped back and looked down at the ground.

"Forgive me."

Eli lifted my chin with the gentleness of a lover's touch.

"Is there a future here for me, Cora?"

Warmth and excitement rushed through my body. My thoughts reminded me I'm not worthy of Eli's affection. Wait. What kind of lie was that? Maybe, just maybe, there could be a chance.

"Maybe so."

"Wouldn't that be fine? Let's head on up to the house."

"Yes, my dear."

A grin grew across Eli's face, It grew until his smile shone like the sun on a hot summer's day.

"Well, I'll be," Eli said while a dash of hope entered his grief. "Let's head up for something to eat."

Eli waved his arm, pointing the crowd toward the house. Friends from church and Negro community leaders lauded Hattie's service. Her work helped many.

After the upheaval of Mama's death and funeral, I walked by the river and experienced the familiar smell of the ground and the sound of water flowing. Trees shaded the spot where I met Janene and Amadahy. How odd that I was there days ago with two women from other times, my timeless sisters. I gave mind to what they told me. Janene told me it wasn't my fault.

I felt I was not worthy of true love since the day that man did unspeakable things to me. He robbed me of my family and so much more. But, that awful time doesn't make me unlovable. Jesus washed me clean. If I'm good enough for Jesus' love, maybe Eli could love me too.

I walked home with renewed hope and happened upon Meriday working in the kitchen.

"Hello, sister. I appreciate you so."

"It's no bother," Meriday said. "Why such a smile on a day like today?"

"I've been thinking."

"What about?"

"About Eli."

"I'm thankful he got to see Mama before her passing," Meriday said.

"Yes. Do you think Eli will settle here and marry?"

"I'm sure he had plenty of prospects in Ashville at the time and returned home without a wife. So, I can't say for sure. Maybe he prefers to remain unburdened."

"Unburdened, yes. But lonely," I said.

"Do you plan on keeping his company?"

"Hush, Meriday. You know I'm not that kind of woman."

"Maybe it's not too late for you and Eli. You've passed your prime. But, I reckon he has too."

"Do you think it's too late?"

"No. He's been pining after you all these years."

"I hope it's not too late."

"Are you sweet on Eli, Cora?"

"I always have been. But, I didn't feel worthy of a man like Eli."

"Of course you are. What changed your mind?"

"Let's just say I've had a change of heart."

"Good afternoon," Eli said as he approached us. "Cora, I'd like to move into Mama's room if you have no objections."

He didn't own much more than some tools and a change of clothes. From the looks of his clothes, I was sure he had not been courting. I hoped to find time to sew him new britches.

"I think that is a fine idea. Let me help you get settled."

"Much obliged," Eli said as he carried his pack to Hattie's room. I followed. Hattie's scent lingered in the room, confronting me with grief. My gaze landed on Eli's profile while he opened the shutters. He looked as handsome as he did the day he found me under the tree all those years ago. Time and labor left creases behind. I fell on the bed as sorrow caused my legs to buckle.

"What's troubling you?" Eli asked as he helped me sit up.

"What am I going to do without Mama?" I said, choking back tears.

"Oh, Cora. I'll be here. I'll be here as long as you need me." Eli lifted me and put his arms around me.

"Please stay," I said and sank into his embrace.

"Do you want to keep the children here?"

"Yes. Not only do I want to care for the children we have, but I also want more. I want a house fit to care for them. We can call it Hattie's House."

"Hattie's House. That's a fine name. If I had the lumber, I could build Hattie's House for you and the children."

"I think I have a plan. Once, I tried to register the orphanage with the State of North Carolina. But they said no to me, a Negro woman. But, the letter said a white man could, and I know a white man who can help us."

"How, in God's name, do you know a white man? A white man who will help you? I never," Eli said with a mix of surprise and confusion.

"It's a long story. Never you mind."

"Well, I do mind. You must tell me, Cora."

I was terrified to tell him. No way he would marry me if he knew the truth. Should I lie? I can't let Hattie down. I can't give up on my dream.

"I went to a white church in town, asking for help with taking care of the children, and a man agreed to help us. He sends money every month."

"For what in return?"

Eli stood up and walked toward the window.

"Why would he give money to someone he doesn't know? How do you know him?"

"It's not important, Eli."

"What are you hiding from me? I must know. You must tell me."

I hung my head, ashamed, and afraid.

"He hurt me. He and the men traveling with him killed my family. I ran, Eli. I ran away as fast as I could. It wasn't my fault, don't think badly of me," I said sobbing.

I pulled my knees to my chest and looked away, faint-hearted.

"Was that when Lewis and I found you?"

I shook my head, yes. I felt Eli's heavy breath on my neck, I released my legs and turned to see engorged veins pulsating in his throat.

"Who is he? Where is he? I'll hunt him down," Eli said with spit flying from his mouth.

"He's no use if he's dead," I said as I brushed my hands down his arms in an attempt to calm him. I'd never seen him this angry before. "Let's turn what was meant for harm into good."

"There's no good in such a man. I'd as soon kill him than rely on him."

"Maybe there's another way. I'll be back in a minute."

Memories of Mama met me in the kitchen. I recall the time Mama made biscuits and gravy for the hungry soldiers that passed through town. She stood up to the commander with humor and bravery. Hattie wasn't about to let them take advantage of her. She also loved that sick baby like he was her own, sacrificing her own life to comfort him in his last days. She taught me how to live with grace and dignity in an unjust world, much like Jesus did.

I looked out the window and surveyed the farm. Mama brought life to this place as sure as April brought spring showers. Children worked and played, learned and grew, arrived and moved on. Chickens pecked the ground, and horses stared at the ground, hoping for hay to appear. Younger children played near the barn as older ones tended to their chores. This place was full of life and a safe place for many.

Eli joined me in the kitchen, calmer than before yet, his fists held clenched.

"Who is he, Cora? I need to know who hurt you, and who killed your family."

"It's Deacon Horton, down at the white church in town."

I regretted telling Eli the second the words tumbled out of my mouth.

"Don't do anything rash, Eli. Let the Lord take revenge for Deacon Burton's evil deeds," I said as Eli rushed out the door. I feared my words didn't lessen Eli's fury.

Eli returned after dark. I hugged him, sinking my head into his chest, relieved he came home unharmed. Eli lifted my head and held my face with both hands. "He won't hurt you no more, Cora. Never again."

I walked away and busied myself in the kitchen.

"I saved you some supper, it's still warm."

"I'll eat later. Come on back here. I need to talk to you."

I walked toward Eli with my heart aching in fear. "What is troubling you, dear?"

"Come sit by me," Eli said, patting next to him on the

wooden bench. "I'm not troubled, I love you so, Cora. I've loved you as my sister, and now, I'm in love with you as a grown woman. I want to spend all my days with you."

He picked up my hands and held them in his.

"Will you marry me? I promise to take care of you and all the children. We can build Hattie's House together."

Fear left me, and my heart filled with love and acceptance I'd dreamed of since I was a child.

"Yes, Eli, yes. I'd be honored to be your wife."

We embraced, and I fancied the hope of our future.

CHAPTER NINETEEN

Amadahy

Aguaquaria
Harvest Moon, 1664

Walking, I am listening to a deeper way. Suddenly
all my ancestors are behind me.
Be still, they say. Watch and listen. You are
the result of the love of thousands.
— Linda Hogan

I awoke to feel a cold, wet feather sweeping across my fore-head. I didn't want to open my eyes and leave this tranquil state. My timeless sisters. It seems like we have similar pain remedied by gratitude. It's true for people across all lands.

"Amadahy, wake up. Show me you're awake," Quatsey said.

"Mama, the sun is high. Get up, please."

The feather stopped, replaced by someone with small hands shaking my shoulders. I made a choice to wake up after hearing Leotie's voice. I put my hands and feet flat on the mat to ground myself.

"I'm awake little one." I opened my eyes and said, "You're not little anymore."

"Little or big, that's not important. I need you here, Mama."

"I'm here. I'll never leave you. You're more important than

the sun."

"May I be your moon?" Quatsey asked.

I sat up and extended my arms, wanting to embrace them both.

"Quatsey, I'm happy to see you here in my village."

"I felt lonely when you left. It felt like you were a full moon's journey away from me. I missed you both."

Leotie smiled as she felt included and squealed with delight. "Can we go for a walk through the meadow?"

I looked at Quatsey to see if she wanted to go.

"I think it's a wonderful idea to return to the place where we first met."

The three of us walked through the meadow, greeted by lavender. Leotie ran ahead with the sun and breeze dancing in her hair. Quatsey reached for my hand, and I consented with a squeeze. Something felt different in my spirit. My life, before meeting my timeless sisters, whirled like the wind. I longed for peace and acceptance yet, remained empty. I needed to rid my life of shame and suffering. Was it now possible to be free? Maybe Quatsey was a gift from the Great Spirit. I'd never felt such contentment.

We walked to the river and sat among the riverbed rocks. Leotie played, her toes splashing in the water. Quatsey and I sat in silence. No words could express my thoughts.

"May I explore?" Leotie asked.

"Where are you going?" I asked.

"I will follow the riverbank to the south."

"Watch your footsteps, and stay close."

"Yes, Mama."

Leotie walked away, and I turned my attention to Quatsey. I gazed at her beauty, strong arms, long legs, and smooth, round breasts. A warm sensation washed over me.

"I'm glad you're here."

"I felt sad when you left my village."

"Leotie and I didn't want to leave. We enjoy being with you."

I leaned into Quatsey, feeling her warmth. She ran her fingers through my hair. Anticipation hung in the air as we watched the river water flow downstream. What will become of us?

"Daylight is leaving," Quatsey said. "Leotie hasn't returned. Should we search for her?"

"She knows this land well. I'm not worried; she will return soon."

Quatsey and I embraced, and I felt warm again, but this time, it rushed through me like lightning. We waited for Leotie, but she didn't appear.

"Let's return home and prepare a meal," I said.

My home carried the scent of my foremothers; smoke, pelts, and wafts of lavender. Dusk peeked through the door as a loud screech interrupted the serenity.

"Who dares enter? Get out! Get out!"

I found Mother crouched in the corner like a wolf cornered in the rocks. Fear covered her face, and her dark eyes looked right through me. I wonder if my father fled the village with my brothers to protect them from her, their mother.

"Mother, it's me, Amadahy. There's no need to worry."

"Oh, dear. Why do the men torment me? They are coming to kill me."

"Who is going to kill you?"

"The Long Hair men. They want me dead."

"No one is going to kill you, Mother."

"You know nothing. A man from the Long Hair Clan has put an evil spirit in my body. You're as dumb as the day you were born."

"Why, Mother? Why would he do that?"

"I possess the knowledge they want, and I won't give it to them, never."

"You're safe now."

I looked at Quatsey to see her reaction. She shrugged her shoulders and grimaced.

"I'm sorry, Quatsey. She's been troubled since I was born. She means no harm."

"It must be difficult for both of you. I wish I could help."

"It helps to have you here."

"I'm worried about Leotie. Shouldn't she be home by now?" Quatsey asked.

"Yes, but she knows this land well. She's probably following a butterfly. I won't worry until the sun sets."

We fed Mother some dried meat and rubbed water on her face, attempting to wash away her fear. She fell asleep peacefully with her head on my lap. I stroked her hair and turned my attention to Quatsey.

"I see you are using your new baskets," Quatsey said.

"Yes. I'd like to learn more from you."

"I can stay and teach you more."

"Leotie and I would love for you to stay."

"Speaking of Leotie, I am worried about her. The sun has set, and she hasn't returned."

"You're right, she should be home now," I said.

We covered Mother with a woven blanket and set out to find Leotie.

"Let's start at the lavender field and follow the riverbank south," I said.

Quatsey slung her quiver and bow over her shoulder and followed me to the riverbank. The earthy smell brought hope that we were one step closer to finding Leotie.

"Let's follow the riverbank. Look for fresh footprints leading into the brush, Leotie may have gone into the forest," I said.

We walked out of my village into other's lands with no sight of Leotie. I heard a twig snap and signaled Quatsey to stop. My legs shook as memories of the curious bear entered my mind. I turned around to find Quatsey squatted with an arrow loaded in her bow, scanning the brush. She's a warrior, I thought as a smile rose across my face. I nodded, leaving Quatsey in control. She motioned to me to lower myself to the ground, and I complied, knowing she would keep us safe.

We waited, listening to the leaves dancing in the breeze and crickets singing. I wished life was that simple, existing in perfect harmony with the ground. Why did I complicate the natural balance of life?

We waited, low to the ground. Quatsey inched closer to me until her arm brushed against mine. I saw her chest expand as adrenaline-fueled her breath and excitement temporarily replaced my fear. I peered above the brush without seeing a threat and looked to Quatsey. She surveyed our surroundings with her head held high and listened. She looked at me and shrugged, there was nothing apparent to concern her.

We continued looking for signs of Leotie by the moon's light. My feet chilled on the muddy path. We found a fresh beaver carcass, probably left by a satisfied bear cub. The sound of the river current became too loud to alert us to sounds of danger, so we walked west toward a valley.

Quatsey grabbed my arm, signally me to stop. She moved her ear forward with her hand to hear a distant sound.

"A horse, nothing of concern," Quatsey said.

"I'm tired; it's no use to search for her in the dark. Let's stop and rest in the grass. We can continue at dawn when the sun rises in the east," I said.

"What about your mother?"

"She will fend for herself."

I knelt down and made a clearing in the grass. We lay down together and rested in silence. I crept closer to Quatsey until I felt the touch of skin.

"The night is cold, may I lie next to you for warmth?"

Quatsey unfurled, inviting me to enter her embrace. I slid over to her open arms and positioned my back to her chest. She leaned into me, and I felt her spirit dance with mine.

We awoke at dawn to the sound of birds singing. A white-winged dove perched on a high branch, cooing. I pictured its long tail feathers hung in my ceremonial headdress. A beautiful, painted bunting flew by with a blade of grass in his beak. His feathers were painted with colors found in a rainbow. Leotie's absence interrupted the tranquility.

"Quatsey, wake up," I said as I shook her shoulders. "We have to find Leotie. I can't bear to lose another daughter."

"I'm awake. I'll be back."

Quatsey walked into the brush to relieve herself. I sat and contemplated what to do. She came back and asked, "Should we go home and see if Leotie returned?"

We began our journey home. Home - Quatsey said home. I felt hopeful that Quatsey thought my house was her home, as well. We returned home and found Mother eating corn mash.

"Good morning, Amadahy. Who is that?" Mother asked, pointing at the door.

"That's Quatsey, the basket weaver and my friend."

"Friend? You don't have any friends."

"She's a new friend, Mother. A kind and generous friend." I reached for Quatsey's hand and drew her near. "I want to be happy on this journey, Mother. It's what I deserve, and Quatsey brings me happiness."

"You are a strange one, Amadahy."

"Think what you want of me, it's not my concern. More importantly, have you seen Leotie?"

"Not since she left with you. Why? Is she missing?"

"She left us to explore the river yesterday, and we haven't seen her since. I'm worried."

"She's not here. Let's go back and follow the river until we find her," Quatsey said as she checked her bow and arrows.

"I'll pack some dried meat and fruit," I said.

"Move with purpose," Quatsey said.

I gathered enough food for several days and said to Mother, "We will return when we find Leotie."

Quatsey and I gathered our supplies and walked back to the river. Worry captivated me. Every movement of the sun lessened the possibility of finding Leotie alive. I hoped she was safe and not afraid.

Great Spirit, clear my eyes so I can see. Clear my mind so I can direct my energy toward her like a gust of wind. Allow Leotie to feel safe, protected like a bear watches over her cubs.

Every sound caught my attention, the flowing river, the grass swaying. Where had she gone? Who or what took her captive? In my mind, I saw a brown bear dragging her to his den. I saw her floating down the river, I saw a man taking her back to his village. No. She belongs with me. I hid my fear and tears inside.

"We're going to find Leotie, she will return home with us today," Quatsey said as she stopped and looked east, her head held high. "Follow me."

Home. Home safe, the three of us. Quatsey's confidence strengthened me. I'd follow her anywhere. We walked, and I called out her name, "Leotie, Leotie!" Quatsey signaled me to be quiet.

"We are entering the territory of the Long Hair Clan. We can go to their village and ask if anyone has seen Leotie, but we must enter respectfully."

We left the riverbank where a trail blazed through the grass. The sound of my footsteps steps crept up my spine, pounding in my ears like ceremonial drums. Where was my Leotie? My legs never felt weaker, my stomach more upset, my spirit more restless, as we walked toward the village. Quatsey motioned at me to stop as she listened.

"We are close. I hear men talking."

Four men approached us with bows drawn, ready to defend their lives and village.

"What business do you have here?" the eldest man asked.

"I am Quatsey, a basket weaver of the Bear Clan. This is Amadahy from the Wolf Clan village to the north. We are looking for a lost girl named Leotie."

"Welcome. Follow me."

We followed the men to the village and into a tribal meeting, where the villagers encircled the leaders. I scanned the faces and didn't see any signs of Leotie.

The older man spoke to Quatsey and asked, "What is your relation to the missing girl?"

"She's my daughter. Have you seen Leotie? Please tell me she is safe."

Quatsey grabbed my arm and pulled me back behind her. "Patience, Amadahy. Let me lead." I relented and trusted Quatsey to find Leotie.

"The young one didn't return to our village last night, and we are looking for her. Please, could you tell me if you've seen her."

My chest pushed into my throat, and my knees trembled in anticipation as I waited to hear news of Leotie. Quatsey patted my arm in assurance. I was thankful she was with me. It was not like me to rely on someone else for help, but trusting Quatsey agreed with my spirit.

"Wait here," the man said as he walked toward the villagers.

My throat tightened when I scanned the tribe and saw Waya. Anger rose from within me, and I attempted to swallow my sorrow. I held no respect for Leotie's father.

"That's him," I whispered to Quatsey.

"Who?"

"Waya, Leotie's father."

"That's good. If Leotie is here, we know she's safe," Quatsey said.

"I don't trust him."

"Wait for the man to return."

I wanted to run to Waya and beg for Leotie's return, but I knew to follow what Quatsey said. A different man approached as the crowd dispersed.

"My name is Mohe, are you the mother of Leotie?

"Yes."

"I found her sleeping under a tree."

"Thank you. Is she unharmed?"

"Yes, I will take you to her now."

We followed Mohe, eyed by suspicious villagers. Mohe stopped and extended his arm toward a door, "Please enter." Quatsey and Mohe followed me inside. I ran to Leotie and wrapped my arms around her, and inhaled the scent of grass and trees.

"I'm here, Leotie, Mama is here."

I rocked her in my lap and ran my hand down the back of her hair. "Are you hurt?"

"No, Mother. Mohe found me again."

"Again?"

"Yes, he found me and Ahyoka the time we were young and swept down the river. Remember?"

"I do remember," I said, looking into Mohe's eyes. He looked familiar. "How can I ever return the kindness?"

"There is one thing you can do, help me find my mother. My brother and I know that our mother is from the Wolf Clan in the village to the north. Isn't that your village?"

"Yes. What is your mother's name?" I asked.

"I'm not sure what she is called. I don't even know if she is alive. After my father's death, I asked the Elders if they knew of my mother. One said she died; another said she acted crazy like an injured animal. But, both were certain she was of the Wolf Clan."

"Mohe, I know your mother, her name is Unastisgi. She is alive, and she is my mother, too."

CHAPTER TWENTY

Hannah

Westbrook, North Carolina
2015

I know for sure that love saves me and
that it is here to save us all.
— Maya Angelou

I picked up my phone to text Mom and put it down, re-membering she was gone. Losing Mom left a haunting presence, I couldn't escape. Yet, I had no choice but to move on without her. She taught me well, through her life and death, how to live my best experience regardless of cir-cumstance. I feel compelled to honor her life by living as she did.

A few months after the funeral, Dad asked me to sort through her belongings. Happy memories peered through my grief as I caught a hint of her fragrance or the feel of a blouse. I found an old, wooden box and lifted the small, metal latch that secured her secrets inside. An envelope was on top with the name Tom written in Mom's handwriting. I carefully drew out the letter from the unsealed envelope. My con-science reminded me that I shouldn't read it, but curiosity won. I opened the letter and read Mom's last words to her husband of 25 years.

Dearest Tom,

If you're reading this, I've left this life without you. I'm sad to leave but confident you will continue to live a good life until the day we meet again. As I reminisce about our life together, I feel joy, gratitude, and love. I knew I'd love from the day I saw I first saw you on campus. You carried yourself with a quiet spirit that drew admiration and respect. Your intelligence, good looks, and athletic prowess were a bonus. You checked all my boxes for the man I wanted to marry.

We started with just enough money to make ends meet in the apartment we shared with the cockroaches. Love, hope, and dreams compensated for what we lacked in resources. No matter our circumstances, we found friends and fun as our family grew. You were the husband and father of every woman's dreams. Thank you for being there and making sacrifices so we could have a happy family. I'm forever grateful.

The last few years have been beyond difficult. I saw the sadness in your eyes as you couldn't protect or save me from the ravages of ALS. Yet, you protected and cared for me better than I thought possible. Even as I suffered, you carried me through the hardest times. Thank you.

Now, as for the future, give yourself permission to rest and grieve. Then, I want you to enjoy our children and grandchildren to come. It's okay to be happy and be hopeful. Engage in the life you desire and deserve. You have my permission, if you need it, to date and remarry if you find someone who will make you happy. It's what I want for you.

I didn't want to leave you, but I had no choice. Please know I died in peace, and I'm no longer suffering. I want nothing more than for you to know you are a great man and have a future ahead of you.

All my love for eternity,
Janene

My chest heaved as I wiped my nose with my sleeve. I can't believe my mom wanted my dad to remarry. It's too soon to imagine Dad with another woman. No way. I can't imagine. I am thankful, though, for how they have shown me what it takes to keep a marriage alive. It's not always perfect; there are good times and bad. Yet, in the end, love and respect win.

With a twinge of guilt, I folded Dad's letter and returned it to its envelope. I turned the envelope over and ran my hands across Mom's beautiful writing. I remember how the birthday cards and personal notes impacted me. I felt her love through them. I looked back in the box and found two more envelopes. One addressed to Daniel and one to me. I picked up Daniel's and couldn't resist.

Dear Daniel,

I'm writing this, so you will know how much I love you. You're a man now, but you are still my baby, always and forever. Nothing can change that. My heart filled with joy when you entered this world and completed our family.

As a baby, you smiled at everyone, and no one could resist your chubby cheeks. Hannah's attention invoked your cutest belly laughs, and hunger was the only disrupter of your content. Relentless curiosity and movement defined your toddler years. You preferred discovering how things work rather than schoolwork. Playing football saved your high school career. You only have a few years left before you strike out on your own.

Here are a few things I need you to know:

1.   You are responsible for your happiness. Don't relinquish your power to another person or circumstance.

2.   Remember, you are a powerful, talented, intelligent, caring, and handsome young man. Mama said.

3.   Find a career that aligns with your passion. Don't settle for less.

4.   Marry a partner who loves you as much as I do and build a family together. Don't settle for less.

5.   Learn early that relationships, people, and peace are more important than money or social status.

6.   Serve your community. It's important.

7.   And finally, be grateful. It's the surest way to stay present and enjoy every moment.

Wherever life takes you, know that I am watching over you with pride. Life is a bumpy ride, and I am confident you have the strength and wisdom to tackle the hard times and enjoy the good times.

I am proud of you, son. Grieve my passing as you see fit, then honor my life by living your best life. Think of me when you graduate, marry, and become a dad. I'll be there. Say hi when you think of me. Talk to me about the decisions you need to make or when you want to share some news. I'll listen.

I love you more than words can express,
Mom

Wow. Mom loved him. I know Daniel is going to miss his biggest cheerleader; She encouraged him at every turn. I hope he stays sober through his grief. Mom would turn over in her grave if he didn't. I returned Daniel's letter to its envelope and looked at mine with anticipation. What were Mom's last words to me? I held the message to my face and inhaled.

My Dearest Hannah,
It breaks my heart that you have to read this letter. I, too, lost my mom too soon. I know it leaves a hole in your heart as you think about times I'm supposed to be there with you. The pain lessens over time but never goes away. All I can ask is that you honor my life by living your best life.

I remember the day you came into this world and made

me a mom, loving you lessened my lack of confidence. Thank you for starring in the best day of my life. You were a carefree baby. Good thing Daniel came second, if he had been the first child, we may not have had a second. I'm joking, of course. No, I'm not.

I felt life anew watching you explore with imagination and curiosity. Life is more fun seeing through the eyes of a toddler. As you grew, you spent much of your time in your head, contemplating how the world works and why people do the things they do. Curiosity fueled your desire to be an anthropologist. Follow your passion in whatever you do.

Forgive me if I skewed your perception about what is valuable. It's nice to look beautiful on the outside, but it's more important to feel beautiful on the inside. Embrace yourself just as you are and focus on who you want to be. You are wise beyond your years. Listen to Spirit, not to society, and share your gifts with the world when ready.

Thank you for sacrificing your plans to care for me. I treasured our time together. I never felt like a burden, only loved. Now it's time for you to make yourself the priority. Get your degree and maybe find your life partner. Now, about that. Find a partner who makes you a better person, someone who loves you like your dad, and I do. Don't settle for less. Find your tribe, people who love and support you and reciprocate. I'm grateful that we were part of the same tribe. I will be with you always. Talk to me when you need a listening ear. I'll hear you.

All my love,
Mom

PS. I left you our sacred talisman that connects you to the collective sisterhood. You'll know when it's time.

ABOUT THE AUTHOR

Shelly Hoover, Ed.D. is an educator and advocate for people living with ALS. She lives with her husband, Steve, in Northern California. Email shelly@shellyhoover.com to receive free book discussion questions or visit shellyhoover.com.

◆ ◆ ◆

Made in the USA
Monee, IL
14 May 2021

68619620R00111